ALL
IS
FORGIVEN

Also by Linda L. Russo

Diary of a Court Reporter with George B. Blake

The Decline and Fall of the US Empire with Joseph Pappy

Cook Italian with Me

LINDA L. RUSSO

ALL
IS
FORGIVEN
MEMOIRS OF A KILLER

Cover design by Joshua Rafols
Interior design by Jake Muelle

ISBN: 978-0-99958-580-1
Fiction / Thrillers / Crime

16.05.12

Dedicated to my son, Joe, whose love and understanding I could not live without; to my daughter-in-law, Heather, whose patience makes me love her more and more every day; and to my grandchildren, Isabela and Max, whom I love with all my heart. I promise I will never say no.

Contents

Introduction

Scottsdale, Arizona

I t was ten thirty at night. The streets of Scottsdale were quiet. The home that I lived in when I was married to Scumbag, my second husband, consisted of three bedrooms, two baths, a family room with tile floor, a built-in bar, and a large fireplace. Oh, so many wonderful memories of parties in this room with family and close friends. There was a big pool in the backyard. Beyond the pool was the desert. You could hear the coyotes howling at night. No neighbors were outside.

The lights were on in the house. *Perfect. My ex-husband was home*, I thought. I drove around the block and parked the car. With the hood of my sweatshirt up so nobody would recognize me if they came out, I walked back to the house and rang the doorbell.

I could hear footsteps walking toward me. I knew he was home, so I had my gun with the silencer attached, ready to kill.

He opened the door, and I could see the shocked expression in his eyes as I pulled the trigger and said to him, "All is forgiven."

1

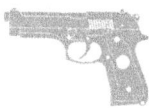

Growing Up in Peterstown

Let me start at the beginning. My name is Sara. Sara Bocelli—no relation to Andrea Bocelli, the wonderful singer. I was born and raised in a small town in Jersey called Peterstown, or the Burg, as the Italians call it. It was a small community. All Italians.

It wasn't crowded. There were a lot of empty lots. We all knew each other. That is, all our parents knew each other. So when we were born, all the kids were introduced to each other from birth, and we all remained friends throughout our lives. Wherever life would take us through the many years, we knew we could always count on each other for support.

It was a typical Italian neighborhood. The men, our fathers, would meet at the Italian American Club at night and play cards, while the women, our mothers, took care of the children and the home. My uncle had the candy store on the corner next to our house where all the guys would hang out, just hanging, doing nothing in particular. Standing on the street corner talking, smoking cigarettes, joking around, singing. Next to the candy store was an empty lot and then the barber shop and then the Amoco gas station, which backed up into our yard, with a small barn and horses. And across the street was The Silver Moon, a bar-restaurant.

Mario, Bobby, and Al lived next door to us on the right, and after school, Mario and I would meet on the back porch and draw for hours. "Mario, you did it again! Look at what you drew! Look at what I drew! Why is yours so nice and mine is so ugly?" And I'd rip my drawing up and storm home.

Well, needless to say, Mario went on to become a very famous artist. We still keep in touch with each other, but I gave up drawing.

I learned how to count at home in our kitchen. Yep, one meatball, two meatballs. And as I got a little older, my mom was teaching me how to make gravy and meat-balls. By this time, I knew how to count, and my girl-friend, Carol, was at the house. She dropped a meatball on the floor, we picked it up, brushed it off, kissed it up to God, and threw it back in the pot. But as we were stirring the tremendous pot of gravy, we looked at each other in utter amazement.

"What in the world is this?" I asked her.

We fished it out of the pot. "Where did this can come from? Hide it before your mother comes in," she said.

We had no crime in our neighborhood. The men were too busy robbing and killing everybody else, but kept us safe. We were so safe that in the summertime, we would sleep on our screened-in porch in front of the house and nobody would disturb us. As the neighbors would walk past our house to go to the candy store, they'd see us outside and stop to say hello and gossip.

"Did you hear Lenny has the flu?"

"No. And I kinda wish I didn't know it now. I was out talking to him yesterday. Hope I don't catch it."

My mom and dad had four daughters. I was the youngest. My dad had nine brothers and sisters, and they all had kids, my cousins, and we all lived in the same neighborhood. My dad always wanted a boy, but after I was born, I think he gave up hope, so he got a dog and named him Junior. We played hide-and-seek with Junior, and little by little, Junior took over the neighborhood. Eventually, he would walk me to school, which was a block away, hang out on the corner with Whitey the Cop, and then walk me home after school. Junior would take his naps in the middle of the street, and guess what? The neighbors drove around him or went down a different street so they didn't disturb him. Sure, they could kill people but not dogs. Not Junior anyway.

My oldest sister, Gina, played the piano. I just love the piano. I tried and tried but just could not succeed, so I would sit after school and listen to her practicing.

We were such a close family, and one Mother's Day, my dad presented my mother with four hundred tulips! All were with different colors, and they were beautiful. They were my mom's most favorite flower in the world. But my big sister, Gina, was laughing so hard that I had to ask, "Gina, why are you laughing at Daddy?"

Gina whispered in my ear, "Daddy lost all his money playing cards last night and didn't have anything for Mom for Mother's Day, so he brought me to the park last night, and with two pairs of scissors, we cut all the tulips in the park so he could give them to Mommy." Of course, it made the headlines in the local newspaper... they were looking for the thief!

As long as we're on the subject of Gina, let me tell you a story. My dad worked in the lab for a local oil company, whose name we shall not mention, and was under contract with them. He made up this concoction in the lab and named it "Glo" because it would clean dishes and make them "glow." It was dishwashing detergent. He couldn't patent it because of the contract with the oil company, but at night, we would all get together and make up this concoction in our basement, bottle it, and give it to all my aunts and uncles.

Uncle Skippy and Aunt Jenny, my mom's sister, used to come to our house every day, along with Uncle Frankie, one of my dad's younger brothers, and Aunt Sally. Uncle Jimmy, another one of my dad's younger brothers, lived downstairs in our basement that consisted of his bedroom and bath, a kitchen, washroom, and a gigantic recreation room with a built-in bar. We were a very close family. Uncle Jimmy used to go to Florida on vacation, and one year he brought back a monkey! He was the most adorable little guy you ever saw, and we dressed him up every day and played games with him.

One day while walking to the store with Uncle Skippy, we heard a noise, and Uncle Skippy said, "Keep your eyes straight ahead, babe." And of course, I listened to everything Uncle Skippy told me to do. But when I woke up the next morning, I heard there was a man lying in the gutter dead. I heard talk afterward that he was just walking through the neighborhood and that he got into a fight with one of the guys. No strangers walked through our neighborhood. There was no reason for a stranger to be in our neighborhood. In fact, the police didn't even come into our neighborhood. They made a U-turn and went the opposite way.

We never had to go out of the Burg to go to the store because we had an Italian grocery store and bakery close by that carried everything we needed. The lady at the bakery was so intimidating when you would go in to buy bread. If she didn't know you or didn't like you, you got nothing. She'd stand there and point, "There's bread for you, you, and you, but no bread for you." You didn't dare say anything, or you would be excommunicated from Fourth Avenue.

Then we had the lemon ice stand on one corner. There was an ice house and another Italian restaurant on the corner of Third Avenue and High Street. If you're sitting at a table in the back of the restaurant and wanted to go into the bar, you had to walk through the kitchen. But everybody knew you, so it was okay.

One day, our grocery store was out of biangoline— pronounced "bee-ung-a-leen"—and my mother told me and my older sister, Gina, that we had to go to the big grocery store, which was outside of the Burg, because she needed biangoline. So my sister got the keys to the car, the money, and off we went, driving outside our neighborhood. Scary thought.

We finally pulled in front of the store and couldn't find a parking place, so my sister gave me the money to go inside *alone* while she waited outside. Boy, was I scared. *Going inside this big store all by myself? How will I find my way back out? They should have signs up with directions in a big store like this, shouldn't they? Where's the manager? I'll get somebody to help me.*

I walked up and down the aisles and finally found someone to help me. "Can you tell me where your biangoline is?" I asked. But the guy doesn't know what the hell I'm talking about. "Speak English," he said. *What the hell?* "I am speaking English."

"What do you use this for? Is it some kind of food?"

Is this man serious? I thought. I said, "No, it's not food. Don't you use biangoline? You put it in your wash to make your clothes white." So he started laughing. I wanted to ask him what was so funny.

"Follow me," he told me with a stupid look on his face. "Here, use this. It's called bleach."

"All right, I'll take this home, but if it doesn't work, my mother will be back looking for you, and you better run."

When I went back out to the car and started explaining to my sister what happened, my sister started crossing her eyes. "Oh, are we in trouble." We were afraid to go home, so we stopped for a lemon ice on Fourth Avenue. When we finally had enough courage to go home, we pulled up in front of the house; it was a frightening experience. Mom was waiting for us with the wooden spoon! Mom was about four feet tall, but when she spoke, you listened, or out came the wooden spoon.

I remember one day she pulled this guy, Bobby, out of the car in front of our house when he was parking to go into the candy store because he had gone on a date with one of my sisters. I'll explain that later. But Mom had her cane, which was worse than the wooden spoon. She was waiting on the front porch, cane in hand, and when she saw Bobby pull up, she went down the front steps of our house, walked in front of his car, which he immediately stopped, opened his door, pulled him out of the driver's seat, and beat him with her cane, not saying a word. Of course, everybody in front of the candy store next door saw what was happening and laughed their heads off. Bobby never lived that one down.

So as we brought the bag from the grocery store in the house, Mom was waiting for us.

"Where's the biangoline?" *Oh, s——t.*

"Mom, they didn't have biangoline, but the man said to try this. He said if you don't like it, we can bring it back."

There was a moment of frozen silence. *Oh, s——t.* My sister and I looked at each other, ready to run out the back door. Now anyone with an Italian mother would know to beware. Mom took it ungracefully out of my hands as I started planning my escape route. *How fast can she run with a cane?* I thought, checking the back door to make sure it was unlocked. As she went into the washroom to use the biangoline, I ran out to the backyard, never to be seen again for the rest of the day.

But I survived that and continued to grow and get older, all in the neighborhood. Never had much reason or desire to go outside our close-knit neighborhood where everyone was friends.

Then one day, Aunt Sally came over to talk to me. "Sara," she said, "I'm moving to Phoenix with Sammy and Lorraine."

Tears came to my eyes. "You can't leave, Aunt Sally. I'll miss you too much, and me and Sammy need our peanut butter and jelly sandwiches, and nobody understands me like Lorraine." Lorraine and I spoke pig-Latin to each other. Aunt Sally didn't understand.

The next day, Sammy and I—or is it me and Sammy— packed our peanut butter and jelly sandwiches and ran away to the backyard and hid behind the bushes.

Nobody even realized we ran away. Nobody missed us. Nobody was even looking for us. So when our sandwiches were gone, we looked at each other and thought it best to go inside because it was getting dark. And the next week, they packed their bags and drove to Arizona, and it was a long time before I could eat peanut butter and jelly sandwiches again.

Growing up, I belonged to a gang. Girls and guys. The girls were called the Del Ray Debs, and we had gang jackets to prove it, violet and black were the colors. Watch out, here we come. There was me, Cindy, Janie, Deena, Betty, Annie, and Carol. The guys were Frank, Chaz, Tommy, Mike, Tony, and Angelo. The girls would walk in front, while the guys walked behind us, harmonizing songs and serenading us. We even played leap frog down Amity Street, and when it came time for me to leap over Chaz, I would stop leaping and punch him.

"Bet you can't catch me."

Chaz tried, but I was too quick for him. Boy, did I laugh as I antagonized him. Chaz was so handsome. His family was from northern Italy, and he had blond hair and blue eyes. Chaz would eventually go to the candy store where the guys hung out next door to my house and tell Augie how I picked on him.

Augie was even more handsome. I remember Augie from when I was about seven years old. He had a crush on my sister, Amanda, and she was crazy about him. They were meant for each other. It was one of those things where at ten years old they fell in love and it lasted their whole lives. I remember only one argument they had, and they broke up, and my sister—she was a stinker—wanted to make Augie jealous and went out with Bobby. When my mother found out about it, that's when she pulled Bobby out of the car and beat him with her cane.

Augie eventually married my sister and was welcomed into the family with open arms. But when I would see Augie after teasing Chaz, Augie would say, "Sara, stop picking on Chaz." But it was just something I had to do.

One summer day, me and my sisters—or my sisters and I, however you want to say it—were in the backyard just fooling around, laughing and joking, didn't mean anything by it. The candy store next door was full, and the guys were standing outside because it was a beautiful day, and one of my sisters said, "Let's play a game. Let's close our eyes and throw eggs and see where they end up."

"Mom's going to find out," I told her. "Maybe we better not."

"No, she won't. She's not home. Let's do it."

Yep, raw eggs. We were so bad. So of course, I listened. I was a good girl, a good little sister. We took a raw egg in each hand, closed our eyes, turned around in a circle a couple of times, and threw the eggs. The idiots that we were.

"What the f——? What's this?" We heard somebody scream.

"Uh-oh!" my sister said. "We better hide."

"I think we hit somebody."

"No. Couldn't have," she said.

We immediately ran inside, locked the door, and snuck by the front window so we could hear what was going on. Louie was standing there with raw eggs running down his face.

"Told you," I said.

We hid after that for a week. Needless to say, we learned a new language that day.

In the summertime, we weren't close to a pool, so everyone would go down to the creek—we pronounced it the "crick"—to go swimming. You can't go in it today because it's disgustingly dirty filthy. Or the guys would open the fire hydrant on the street, and we'd run in the water and play.

One Saturday morning, Cindy and Chaz came over with their bats and a—yes, one—ball. "We thought we had nothing to do, so wanted to do something," said Cindy. "So we followed the trail of deception that lead us straight to you."

"What exactly are you suggesting?" I said.

"We're not suggesting anything exactly," said Chaz. "I'm just saying."

This was getting too confusing for an early Saturday morning.

"Want to go to the park and play ball?"

"Well, it's a definite maybe," I said. "Let me make sure I can go." I turned around and saw my mother standing behind me. At least, she didn't have the wooden spoon in her hands.

"Go ahead," Mom said. "But stop at your grand-mother's on the way to the park to see her."

I got my glove, and we walked over to the park, peeked in to see Grandma and Grandpa, and gave them a big kiss—had to bust Chaz a little on the way. I just had to. Grandma loved Chaz and got a big kick out of us teasing him. They were little things, like throwing the ball at him, tripping him.

"*Princesa*," he called me. "Stop that before I tell Augie."

This is going to be fun. Maybe Cindy and I will tackle him and sit on him.

As we were cutting through the flower garden to take a shortcut to the field, Chaz said, "Look over there. Do you see that? What is that?"

The three of us held hands and slowly walked toward something we didn't understand yet couldn't take our eyes off of. As we got closer and closer, it appeared to be…but it couldn't be. We were too scared to stop, so we crept step-by-step, being sure to all hold hands silently as we walked. United we were brave.

"Let's call the police!"

"Let's go to Gramma's!" We ran as fast as we could back to Gramma's to tell her and Grandpop what we discovered.

"Gramma, there's a man hanging in the park. He's dead!"

Well, I guess if he was hanging, he would be dead. It wasn't one of the neighborhood guys. It was a stranger. Grandma and Grandpa called the police, and because they were so nervous, they spoke Italian and tried to convey what we were telling them. They finally got across "dead" and "park," so the police took all that information about the "dead park" and met us back at the park. But I wasn't going back to the park without Grandpa. It sure was something we talked about to everybody afterward. They said that's what he got for walking in the Burg. I hate when that happens. The Peterstown Press printed a big article in the paper about us finding the body.

Did you ever have a conversation with someone and you didn't understand them and they didn't understand you? Well, Grandma and Grandpop didn't speak English, but we could talk and laugh all day long. I just loved them. They were very understanding!

I have to tell you a story about Grandma. One of my cousins just told me this. I didn't know a thing about it. She was born in and lived in Sicily. She started dating a young man whom her family frowned upon. It seems he was of a lower class, and they did not want her to see him. It was a Romeo and Juliet kind of thing where they fell madly in love.

So what did they do? They ran away together and got married. She started having babies, and they decided he would come to the United States, work, and send for her. Her favorite saying was, "I have one in my belly, one in my arm, and one in hand."

To make a long story short, his name was Dominick, he came to the United States, worked, and sent for Grandma and their three children. They moved to "the neighborhood" where he hooks up with the Wise Guys and started gambling. In one of the card games, he got into an argument, and shots were fired from another guy in the room who was a politician. The politician killed the other card player.

Now the captain of the police force in Elizabeth was a personal friend of this politician, and he didn't want to see him get into trouble. He didn't like Dominick, so the police charged Dominick with first degree murder instead of the politician. When they arrested him, he called Grandma and asked her to bring him a box of thirty cigars because he would be out in thirty days and he'd have one cigar each day. Well, that didn't happen. He was tried and was sent to prison. While in prison, the guards tormented him, telling him his wife (Grandma) was cheating on him. He beat some of the guards up; he was a big man, and other guards held him down and beat him, and then they had him transferred to the hospital ward where they performed a prefontal lobotomy, at which time they transferred him to Marlboro, which is a crazy place and where he eventually died.

So then Grandma rented out a room in her house to a man who later became Grandpop, and they had nine more kids. Poor lady.

2

Unorganized Crime

Getting back to the neighborhood, everybody was used to what they call "organized crime." That was a way of life for all of us because the gang didn't know anything different. The men in our neighborhood organized? I thought. That was a joke in itself. They couldn't organize their socks. The Del Ray Debs were more organized than them. And all the men had nicknames. Nobody knew anybody's real name. All nicknames: Gags, Bee-Bee-Gun, Popeye, Billy-the-Kid.

Then there was the ragman on his horse and wagon riding down Fourth Avenue on the cobblestone street. One of my sisters used to help me put on my cowboy boots, and we'd hop over the fence in the backyard to go in the barn and take the horses out for a ride. Boy, I remember when they paved Fourth Avenue—how I cried!

"They're taking out the cobblestones? What about the horses? What about the ragman?" Oh, wait until I tell you about the ragman.

I remember one year they had a meeting in upstate New York, and all the men were going, the older generation men. While up there, there was a police raid, so everyone scattered into the mountains. When one of the "unorganized" men was pulled over by the police, the police asked him where he was going.

"I'm up here looking at property to buy."

"At midnight?" said the police officer.

Needless to say, he was brought in for questioning.

Of course, that didn't apply to my family. My dad was the councilman of our ward, the Fifth Ward, so we were in the middle of everything. One day, I was eavesdropping and heard one of my sisters and my dad talking.

"Dad, can we have a block party? I always wanted to go to a block party. Please, Dad? Please, Dad?"

"I'll see what I can do," my father told her.

I don't know how he did it, but a few months later, he had our street closed off to traffic, had a band playing music, dancing, had all kinds of food, goodies and drinks for the whole weekend, you know, like that big Italian feast downtown New York in Little Italy. And then we had it every year…it was called the Feast of St. Rocco down in Peterstown. And we didn't have to walk anywhere. All we had to do was open our front door.

Middle School and High School

Middle school and high school were a real friggin' pain in the ass. It was rough to get through. We had to go to the outskirts of town—out of our neighborhood a block—to get to middle school. So our gang, the Del Ray Debs, and the guys left Whitey the Cop and would meet on the corner, but Junior couldn't walk me anymore.

"Walking a block out of our neighborhood," I said to the girls. "I strenuously dislike this." (I like that word for a female "strenuously." It's feminine.)

"What's next?" said Janie.

Middle school was rough, but we were growing up, and I guess this was something we had to do. There were so many kids and teachers that the only way I could be happy was singing a song that the girls in our gang, the Del-Ray Debs, had made up about our gym teacher. The guys didn't participate. They were nice. We were mean.

"Glow, little glow worm, scatter, scatter. Miss Sorenson's getting fatter, fatter. Her teeth are false and her hair is peroxide. In the moonlight she looks cross-eyed. Lace on her petticoat blowing in the breezie. I can see her bowlegged kneesie. All the boys say she's taboo. Glow, little glow worm, glow."

As I proceeded to push a girl down a flight of stairs because I didn't like the color of her lipstick on her funny-looking lips, I thought to argue with a fool proves there are two. I didn't understand why, but a riot broke out.

"What's everyone so upset about? She didn't break anything." That day, the police were called in, and all my sisters were waiting outside after school to walk me home.

Years passed, and it was my sixteenth birthday, and my mom planned a Sweet 16 birthday party for me and invited all my close friends and, of course, Junior, our wonderful dog. We were all having such a great time down in our basement in the rec room dancing and then playing spin-the-bottle when all of a sudden Frank, Angelo, and Mike said they had to leave.

"What? Where you going? The party is just getting started."

"Gotta go take care of business," said Frank.

Boy, I thought, *is he going to get it for this.* I found out later that was their first kill. They were making a name for themselves that night. And guess who they friggin' killed? Their first kill was the ragman—on the cobblestone street with his horse and buggy. On my birthday! At least, they didn't kill the horse.

Another year passed, and I was seventeen, learning how to drive. "Don't get in my way, I'll run you down."

First car was from my uncle's junkyard. They fixed up an old Studebaker, and boy, did I love that car. On Thursday nights, the girls would gather in my car, and we'd drive up and down Broad Street, playing the radio loud, of course, singing, laughing. Then all of a sudden, we saw a cop car behind us with its lights on.

"Can't be after me!" I said.

Another couple of blocks, and Cindy said, "What's he doing following us?"

I looked in my rearview mirror. "Okay, sirens on, I better pull over. The nerve of him."

"License and registration," he said.

"Yes, Officer. What could I possibly have done wrong?" I said with an innocently bad mouth.

"There's a lot of oil leaking out the back of your car, and it's smoking."

"I'm so sorry, Officer. I didn't see it."

Then he said, "And you ran a red light."

Well, "I'm so sorry, Officer. I didn't see the red light because there's so much smoke." The girls cracked up. It's a good thing he had a sense of humor. I wound up giving him my phone number and got no ticket in return.

Then there was the night one of my sisters asked me if I ever smoked pot before. "No, did you?" And we decided we were going to try it. But how were we going to try it if we didn't know what to do?

"I know," said my sister, I won't tell you which one. "Clams smokes pot. Let's find him." We were driving down Third Avenue looking for our dear friend, Clams, when we ran into Max.

"Max, have you seen Clams?" said my wonderful sister.

"Yeah, he's either down on John Street or at the Villa Roma with Frank."

We figured we'd check out John Street first because it was closer. We were determined to find him. "Okay, there he is. Clams! We need you." We proceeded to pull up to him, open the back door, and pushed him in the car, kidnapping him. Maybe he won't remember in the morning.

"Clams, you got any pot on you?"

"Oh, baby, do I have pot."

Good enough answer for me. Now, where were we taking him? Couldn't go to the park. I would never go to the park again, and I would never play Hangman again. "So now that we have him, what do we do with him?" I asked my sister.

"Let's take him to Chaz's house," she said.

"You crazy? If his mom comes home, she'll kill us and him. Mom's at bingo. Let's take him down the cellar."

We brought him back to the house, went down the cellar, and searched him. We should have done that when we kidnapped him, but so what? As my sister emptied his pockets and we found what we were looking for, she said, "Okay, Clams, what do we do with this stuff?" He was having a great time. He didn't even realize that we grabbed him off the street and were picking his pockets.

We got it all together and were so excited. We're gonna learn how to roll and smoke pot! Clams showed us. "You gotta do this and this and roll and light and smoke and breathe deep," he said, and we listened and followed everything he told us to do. And we smoked and smoked, but nothing happened!

"Is this all there is?" I said to my sister. We were so disappointed, and then all of a sudden, we heard Mom unlocking the door and coming in the house. Good thing we were down the cellar.

"Clams, get out. Climb out the window." We pushed him out the back window because we didn't want Mom to find us down in the cellar smoking pot. We were so bad.

Drinking Age

The drinking age in Jersey was twenty-one, so on weekends we would sometimes drive over the Goethals Bridge into Staten Island where the drinking age was eighteen. We would drink and dance the whole night long and would have contests—who could pick up the most guys.

One Friday night, Carla, another girlfriend from school, wouldn't come with us. "I have a date," she said. "You'd rather go out on a date on a Friday night than come with us to Staten Island?"

So Cindy, Janie, Deena, Betty, Carol, and I piled into the old Studebaker and drove into Staten Island. *I'll fix her*, I thought. *We're going to have fun tonight.*

Cindy and I were really bad together. This was the night I was going to win the contest. I was going to pick up more guys than ever before, and I was dressing to kill. It was only an immaterial material object, but I wore tight jeans and a sexy shirt.

We danced and danced, and I picked up guy after guy. How I lied…all night long. I even said to one guy, "You are a terrible liar. I like that in a man," trying to cover up some of my lies. I figured I'd call him a liar so he wouldn't call me a liar.

He smiled. "You're crazy," he said laughingly.

"Thanks," said crazy me.

And then when a guy would ask for my name and phone number, I'd say, "My name is Carla Penney," and give them Carla's telephone number. Boy, was I having fun. I won the contest that night.

After that, Carla used to say to us, "All these guys are calling me. I wonder how they got my phone number."

"I know nothing!" said Cindy.

New York City

After high school graduation, I moved to New York City where I managed to get a great job in a law office as a secretary. Hey, this legal stuff is good to know, isn't it? Up to this point in my life, guys were okay, but I just can't find one I really like, I thought. Going to all the clubs in the city, this was my routine. This was my life.

Then one weekend, I got a phone call from a friend I was dating who owned a garbage company in New York. "Hi, Sara, there's a music festival starting this weekend Upstate New York, and we have the garbage contract. Want to go?"

Do I need to tell you what fun Woodstock was? I was never so full of mud in my whole life...while singing, dancing, and holding candles.

When I got back to the city, I needed a little more excitement in my life, and a friend introduced me to Victor Hammond, who owned a big art gallery in the city. His brother was some big wheel in California,

Armani. Victor and I would meet one night a week in a group and go to dinner or do something, hang out at the gallery. Sometimes his friend Huntington joined us. I helped Victor plan the art exhibits and helped send out invitations for private parties to be held the night before the public openings. I didn't accept any money for this work, so Victor started paying me by giving me gifts of art from the gallery. They were beautiful paintings that were treasured.

I finally met the brother, Armani. The story behind their millions was that when they came to New York from Russia on a boat, they brought treasures with them, settled in New York City, and opened up an antique shop. Later on with the money they made from that, they went into art. Armani went to college in NYC and rented a room in a townhouse downtown. After he started making his millions and the townhouse went up for sale, he bought it. A few years later, the townhouse next door went up for sale, and he bought that also, then renovated both, taking down walls and combining them together to make one home. It was beautiful, and the New Year's Eve parties there—what fun.

By this time, I was trying to be attractive and no longer a tomboy. I went out, had a lot of dates, but I still couldn't find anybody I wanted to have a serious relationship with. I kept my weight down, wore short dresses, high heels, let my dark brown, almost black hair grow to my shoulders. And of course, I wore fake eyelashes.

I started dating a guy, but it was nothing serious, and I don't even remember his name—maybe it was Charlie. He was partners with two other fellows, one of whom played professional football, and they owned a bar in New York called The Bachelors.

Charlie would tell me, "Meet me at the bar tonight, then we'll double with Johnny and go to the Copa." My, my, my. Of course. The lines getting into The Bachelors were so long, but the guys at the door would see me and escort me right inside. Oh, what fun.

He was the love of my life that week, but after a while, I got tired of Charlie and threw him away. No more Charlie.

Then one night was the start of it all, my career as a killer. Don't get me wrong, I wasn't a psycho. My first kill was sheer self-protection, but after that, it was for the money. I'm just saying.

There was a party scheduled for the art gallery that we planned and worked hard at, sent invitations to the "important" people in New York City, including a prince. Can't tell you where the prince was from because I'll get sued. The party was a blast. There was champagne, munchies, and more champagne.

The prince was looking better and better. Dance? Why not? The champagne was working, and so was the dancing. I had to stay with Victor to close up shop, but I made a date with the prince for the next evening, Saturday night, at the Plaza Hotel where he was staying. There was a cute nightclub in the hotel, and he would make reservations for us.

The next morning when I woke up, I called my Del Ray Debs girlfriend, Cindy, to tell her about the date I had that night with the prince. "Cindy," I said, "he's a Prince, and we're going out to a show tonight in New York."

"Make sure you call me tomorrow and tell me *all*."

"You bet I will. I'm so excited. Talk tomorrow."

That evening we met in the lobby of the hotel. "You look beautiful tonight," I think he said. With his accent, sometimes I couldn't understand him. We went to the show, had dinner, a few drinks, and were having a won-derful evening. So after the show when I was invited up to see his suite and have a drink, well, how could I turn that down? Of course I'll go up to his suite, have a drink and talk.

How could I be so stupid? I thought later on. We took the elevator to the top floor to his suite. "Oh my, I've never seen such a beautiful hotel suite." And there was a chilled bottle of champagne waiting for us. We talked about the gallery and the people we knew at the open-ing. We talked about living in the United States, drank, talked some more. Little did I know, something was on his mind!

"Sara, come close to me." *What?* I thought. "Come here," he said.

Yes, I was young, stupid, and innocent. *What do I do now? Is this my fault for coming here?* was my thought. *How the hell am I going to get out of here?* As he crept closer and closer to me, my mind kept racing. *Do I scream? Do I try to head for the door? I've never been in this situation before. Maybe I should try to knock the bas-tard out with a sucker punch. But what if he's stronger than me?* As he came closer and closer…

"Please, I don't want any trouble." But the more I pleaded with him, the more intense he got. "I'm just going to leave and forget this ever happened," I told him.

His eyes were shining, his mouth was quivering. The more I spoke, the worse he got. It was an inescapable situation.

He got to his feet, and as he lunged at me, I raised my arms to protect myself, and my champagne glass broke on the table, went up to his neck, and cut his vein. The blood started spurting out. He grabbed his neck and pleaded with me to get him help. As I looked into his eyes, they were no longer shining. His mouth was still quivering but this time in pain.

My training in the law office went to work. As I calmly collected the fragments from the champagne glass and put them in my purse so there were no fingerprints left behind, I looked into his eyes and said, "All is forgiven." Bastard. That was my first kill.

Exiting his room, I walked calmly toward the elevator. I kept my head down and did not make eye contact with anyone as I walked out the front door of the hotel, hoping not to be recognized. I went straight home to my apartment and thought, *What did I do?* Now was the time to get out of town. The next day in the newspaper, it talked about the prince being killed in his suite at the Plaza Hotel, but said that it looked like a ritualistic killing because his throat was cut, and there were no clues left behind. *I'll go into my savings from work*, I thought. Good thing I had been putting money away.

I called Cindy and told her my date was an experience, but I'd be back in Jersey next weekend and tell her all about it.

I had never been on an airplane before, but I needed to leave New York City. I had a friend, another friend named Frank whom I met at the Copa one night, and Frank was about to go back to Caracas, Venezuela, where his family was, so I made it a point to talk to Frank and get invited to Caracas. I was getting good at talking in circles. As it turned out, one of his best friends was a pilot on the Venezuelan Airlines, and I was able to set it up where I would fly to Caracas on one of his flights, and he would drive me to Frank's house after we landed in Caracas.

I gave my two weeks' notice at work, and now I had to go home and tell my mom. That Friday after work, I took the bus out of Port Authority into Elizabeth for the weekend. When I got in, I wondered how I would approach this conversation with my mother. Never mind I just killed somebody for attacking me, but how was I going to tell my mother I was going on a trip…and leaving the country? We sat down.

"Mom, I have a friend who invited me to their house to visit. Is that okay?" This even though I lived in New York City on my own.

"Sure. What time will you be home?"

Oh, boy. "Well, my friend lives outside of Jersey. It's a little place called Caracas." *Oh, boy.*

My mom wasn't too happy about it. When it finally came out that Caracas was in South America, I could see she turned the color purple. But she didn't kill me, so maybe she was getting open-minded at her age. Maybe not.

She said, "Sara, traveling overseas is dangerous. You could get kidnapped and held as a sex slave."

She should know what I just went through. I finally talked her into accepting it and not beating me with her wooden spoon.

Now to meet with the Del Ray Debs to tell them what had happened. I felt like a confidential informant, only I was squealing on myself. I called Cindy, and she called somebody, who called somebody else, and at six o'clock that night, the Debs were in a meeting at the Villa Roma.

"Girls," I said, "we may never be able to meet again," as I explained what happened the weekend before with the prince, but quietly so I wasn't overheard. After the next two hours of pizza, wine, and talk of murder—I felt like I was on one of those mystery rides where you have to identify the killer—we said our good-byes for now, and all promised to stay in touch, and keep our secret.

So the following week, I said good-bye to everyone, all my sisters, Mom and Dad, all my friends in the Burg and told them I'd be back soon, and off I went. I'm sure I could have told them about my "experience," but I chose to keep it quiet. I read in the New York paper about the prince being killed, but as of yet, they had no clues or no suspects.

Travel Time

The flight was pleasant but long. I watched movies and tried to keep my mind off the prince. The pilot friend of Frank's invited me into the cockpit for a while to get acquainted. How the hell do they remember what all these gadgets were for? It was an interesting experience, but I still worried about the prince and the police. I never heard anything more about it, so I guess the police did not suspect me. I was leaving the States in time.

When I arrived in Caracas, I went through Customs, where the pilot was waiting for me, and he drove me to Frank's house. Frank lived with his mother, and she had a gorgeous, beautiful home in the hills.

"Welcome," she said to me. "You're welcome to stay as long as you like." She should know who she was welcoming into her home. Frank showed me the beautiful bedroom I would be using, and I was starting to feel better about the kill. I was starting to feel safer.

I was invited to parties, dinners, dancing. Caracas was wonderful. Frank asked me one day, "Sara, how would you like to go into the Amazon and see the jungle?"

Oh, boy! Headhunters? Imagine if I told my mother about this. "Sure. Why not?" said crazy me. I thought, *This may be the craziest thing I ever did outside of murder.*

We flew into the Amazon on a small private plane and then went on a little boat and then walked. And walked. And walked. But it was absolutely beautiful and peaceful, and I didn't have to kill anyone or anything. We set up a tent and hiked during the day, fished, learned to shoot…just what I needed. At least, I wouldn't have to worry about leaving fingerprints behind. And needless to say, my head wasn't hunted by the headhunters. Did that mean they didn't like my head? Hey, I'm an equal opportunity hater.

After a week, we took our same route back to Caracas.

I had been writing to a girlfriend from New York who was in Spain and after three months in Caracas decided it was time to move on. I didn't spend much money here, thank goodness, because I was staying at Frank's mother's house, and I did have savings from my job, so I made plans to meet my girlfriend in Barcelona, Spain, on a certain date, a certain time at a certain place because I still didn't want to go back to New York.

I left Caracas the following week heading to Barcelona and wrote to my mother so she didn't think I was missing in action. "Sara, as long as you're going to Spain, maybe stop in and see Uncle Pietro in Rome. I'll let him know to expect you."

Well, I thought, *she's coming along.*

The next week, I caught my plane from Caracas to Barcelona, Spain, and there must have been matadors flying on the plane also because they were staging a bull-fight down the aisle of the plane. It was very entertaining. But in the meantime, my friend sent me a letter saying she would be late and asking me if I could wait a week. I didn't get the letter, but I was keeping busy seeing the sights, and I even went to a bullfight after watching the matadors on the plane (which I did not like), and after a few days when my friend didn't show up, I left Barcelona and went to a little town called Torremolinos, Spain, on the Costa del Sol of the Mediterranean. I still didn't want to go back to New York City, although whenever I spoke to Victor, he never mentioned anything about the prince being killed.

One evening, I was eating calamari in an outdoor café in Torremolinos, and when I looked up, I saw in the same café eating calamari my friend Ana. Of course, we both screamed when we saw each other, and we immediately sat together, where I learned about her letter to me explaining that she would be late and asking if I would wait for her.

The next day, we both checked out of our hotels and got on the train to Portugal, where we took a boat to—where else?—Tangiers, Morocco. Yes, Tangiers, Morocco. Don't tell my mother.

When we arrived, we went through Customs, exchanged our money, and met these wonderful guys who worked for the government.

"Where are you girls staying?" Well, what did we know? We didn't think that far in advance.

"Have any suggestions?" said I.

"Yes. We're getting off work and will take you to the Fat Black Pussycat," one of the strangers said to me.

Ana and I huddled a few steps away to discuss our strategy; something that never occurred to us to do was to plan ahead. "Ana, do you think we should trust these strangers whom we never met in our lives to take us to the Fat Black Pussycat in Tangiers, Morocco? Do you think my mother could be right? We could be kidnapped and sold as sex slaves." *They'd be sorry*, I thought to myself.

"Where else would we go? Let's do it," We waved them back into our lives to carry our luggage for us.

We arrived at the Fat Black Pussycat. We checked in while they waited for us, and then we all went out to dinner. After all, I thought, I could always escape back to New York if I had to. But they turned out to be gentlemen, and no violence was needed on our part. The next day, we went to an area called the Petit Socco, which is an open square in the Medina area of central Tangiers, the most interesting, exciting, scariest place I had ever been to.

There were no cars allowed in the Petit Socco area. Only people. Their clothing was called a Djellaba for men and women. "Ana," I said. "Let's be sure we don't lose each other. My mother could still be right."

After three days of that and, of course, going out with our guys, we decided to go to Casablanca, Morocco, so we rented a car and was on our way when we heard on the radio that riots broke out. We made a U-turn and went back to the Fat Black Pussycat and the Medina.

Walking through the Petit Socco was an adventure in itself. There were beggars, singers, thieves, shops, food, everything you could think of. The buildings and streets were run-down, and bricks and concrete were falling apart. The homes looked like they needed so much work on the outside. In the beginning, we were so scared. We were afraid to speak to anyone but just absolutely loved shopping there, so we had to keep going back. I bought a pair of leather slippers for seventy-five cents. I had to go back. Then after a week of walking through the

Medina and seeing the same people, the shop owners, they started saying hello and talking to us, and we
would talk to them. Then one day, one of the shop owners invited us into their home for lunch. We were a little
hesitant, but we still accepted. Once they opened the
door to their home, when you walked inside you'd see
it was a palace. There was gold all over and beautiful
antique furniture. Absolutely magnificent.

After a few more days there and *mingling* (I'm not
crazy about that word; it makes me think of bacteria),
Ana and I started talking about leaving Tangiers and
going back to Europe. So the following day, we packed
our bags, checked out of our hotel, went to the boat dock
where we arrived, and the guys checked us out of the
country. We exchanged our money and got on the boat.
As we were standing there waiting for the boat to fill up
with people and leave, we looked at each other and said,
"Why are we leaving? We're having such a great time.
Do you really want to leave?"

I still wasn't ready to go back and face the consequences in New York City. "No," I said. With that, we
ran off the boat, and the guys checked us back into the
country. We exchanged our money, and they drove us

back to our hotel where we stayed another week. Party time at the Medina!

The following week, it was finally time to leave Morocco, but not head back to New York yet. We were back on the boat to Portugal, back to Spain, and into Paris, France, where we walked down the Champs-Elysees, went to the Right Bank and the Louvre Museum, then to Maxim's to eat, to the Pantheon, and walked over to the Arc de Triomphe. We had an enchanting view from the Eiffel Tower. When we felt we saw enough in Paris, we went to Marseilles, Cannes, the French Riviera, and Nice, where we rented motor scooters to ride around the Riviera. After another month, my friend Ana decided it was time for her to go back to New York City, and I would move on to where else—Italy. After all, I had my Uncle Pietro I had to see and all my cousins in Rome whose address I had. Uncle Pietro owned a bus company in Rome, so off to Rome it was.

When I got off the train in Sunny Rome, it was cold, raining, and I couldn't find my uncle's address. I felt sick to my stomach from something I ate on the train. I looked up and saw one of my uncle's buses because it had his name on the side, and I knew he had a bus company in Rome, so I ran to it, hopped on, and managed to get across to the bus driver, "Take me to your leader." I stayed on the bus to the end, where he actually did take me to his leader—my uncle—in his office. Happiness!

"Sara," said Uncle Pietro as I walked into his office, sick as a dog. "I've been waiting for you."

Uncle Pietro's home was absolutely beautiful. It was three floors with an elevator. I had my own floor, imagine that! My cousins took me sightseeing around Rome for three months. Rome was magnificent. We went to the Vatican, the Colosseum, St. Peter's, the Roman Forum, the Via Veneto, the Tivoli Gardens, the Villa d'Este. We also ate pizza, pizza, and more pizza as we sat by the Fountain of Trevi and then walked the Spanish Steps.

And then one day, we called my mother to say hello and tell her all was well. "Hi, Mom, it's me," I said.

After that call, I missed her so much that the next day I made flight arrangements to go home back to Jersey, where I would try to get another job in New York City and contact my friend, Victor, to tell him I was back in town and maybe try to help out at the gallery again. But this time, I knew better. I wouldn't put myself in that type of situation again. I'm not a killer. Or am I?

No word on the killing or the prince. Was I safe?

Bellevue Hospital

My sister, Liz, had breast cancer previous to this, and she had her breasts removed and in time had reconstructive surgery. So when I came back to the States, we started talking about her health, and she said, "Sara, on Saturday my doctor would like me to go to Bellevue Hospital in New York because they're having an international doctors' conference on breast cancer. He's a speaker there and would like to show the doctors pictures of me when my breasts were removed and what they look like now after reconstruction, but I can't drive, and I don't know my way around the city."

"I can help you if you want to go," I told her.

"Would you be able to drive me to the conference, wait with me at the hospital, and then we'll drive home?"

"Of course," I told her.

So that Saturday morning, we got ready, got in my little red Fiat, and drove into the city. As soon as we were able to park in the hospital's garage, I helped her get out of the car, into a wheelchair, and wheeled her up to the floor where we were going to meet her doctor.

The nurse greeted us and escorted us into a large room to wait for my sister to be called into the conference room. We sat down, and I started looking around the room.

"Liz," I said because that was her name. "Where are we?" Liz was a nurse and she knew *everything*.

"Take a deep breath, Sara. You'll be fine. Don't look around." But the suspense got the best of me.

As I looked around the room and saw a man with no chin, a woman with lumps on her face, and another man with no ears, I lost my heart. My heart just left me in a split second, and I almost fainted. The nurse put me in a wheelchair and moved the two of us to a separate room. I guess Liz's doctor was told because they called my sister into the conference room immediately—with me in the wheelchair—showed the doctors her reconstructive surgery, and then Liz wheeled me out of the hospital, put me in the car, and drove me home!

3

Uncle Tony

Did I introduce you to Uncle Tony yet? And Uncle John? I was closer to Uncle Tony. His nickname was "Cat" only because he owned a panther. He kept the panther in his home, and rumor was that he used it to intimidate and threaten people. He was "Little Cat" and Uncle John was "Big Cat" because he was the older brother.

Uncle Tony ran the Jersey Shore. He was the boss. His right-hand man was Louie with a nickname of "Louie the Killer." Billy the Kid was there, Tommy Feet.

When I got back in the States and back home to the Burg, much to my surprise, I got home in the middle of a mess. Uncle Tony needed help in his office because his secretary left, and he asked me to help out until he could find someone else. "It doesn't look like she's coming back," Uncle Tony said to me.

"You're right, Unk. It doesn't look like it looks like it." *Okay,* I figure, *I have office experience, and I did work for a big law firm, and I love Uncle Tony, even if he was a Wise Guy, but he was organized.* I had heard stories about him and Louie the Killer and what they did to "people who talked," so I figure I'd help out a couple of weeks and stay on the good side of him. I was still afraid to go into New York because of the prince, so I thought this was the safest place for me at the moment. Besides, he trusted me. If he only knew that if anyone in the family was taking after him, it was me. I had heard stories about him and the Wise Guys burning people in his incinerator at his home that were proven to be disrespectful. Wise Guys? Organized? I still couldn't figure that one out.

So I drove down the Jersey Shore to Uncle Tony's where they all welcomed me home, and he asked if I could help him out for a while. "Sure. Why not?" I said.

Uncle Tony was in the building business. I thought I could learn his business and get to meet all the guys involved. So every morning, I would get up, get ready, get in my little Fiat convertible that I had left in Elizabeth, and head on down to the Jersey Shore where I would open up the office if Louie the Killer wasn't there already. After a couple of weeks, I was doing pretty well at handling the calls, scheduling the men, keeping time records.

As I was taking calls one morning and waiting for Uncle Tony to come into the office, Louie and I were there with Louie's cousin, Mutsi, and all of a sudden, who marches in but the FBI. *What? What's happening?* I thought.

"Where's Anthony?" one of them said.

"Who's Anthony?" said smart-aleck me.

"He hasn't come in yet," Louie said.

As I slowly made my way to the window overlooking the front parking area, I figure when he pulled up I'd motion to him to go away. As the FBI came closer to me, I thought of throwing him out the window, but I figured I'd never get away with it.

He said, "Tell us everything you know about Louie the Killer. How did he get his name? How many people did he kill?"

Well, this is simple, I thought. *Why not tell him the truth?* "Sir, you have it all wrong. Louie the Killer got his name because when he was younger, he was so handsome he knocked the girls dead!" I was on the FBI's Most Wanted list after that. I looked out the window and saw Uncle Tony pull in and park. I tried to get his attention to tell him to go away and not come in the office, but it was to no avail. As I was still standing by the window, in walked Uncle Tony. Needless to say, they took him out of there in handcuffs, brought him in for questioning, and he wound up in prison for a number of years because he wouldn't tell them what they wanted to know.

So I was stuck with a job—helping "Louie the Killer" and cousin Mutsi in the office. I got up early every morning and drove down to the Jersey Shore to answer the phone, keep time sheets of the men, and keep the legitimate building business going as much as I could. Every Sunday, Uncle Tony would send the car to pick me up, and I would go to Trenton State Prison to visit. Trenton had no-contact visits. You were on one side of the window, the prisoner on the other, and you would talk through the telephone. Of course, all the discussions were recorded, but I just kept him up-to-date on his building business and what was going on in the office. I told him I loved him too.

It was there in Uncle Tony's office that I met the love of my life. Finally, I can tell you the moment we met. His name was Tony. When he walked into the office, he walked over to me. He smiled. We could not take our eyes off each other. When he spoke, my heart was his. He was working on a building project with Uncle Tony and Louie.

Tony was Italian, of course, and very muscular, very handsome, and very nice. They talked about the project while I sat and watched, listening to his voice. It was *the* moment of my life. *Please ask me out*, I thought.

But he left.

"Sara, can you get Rocky on the phone?" said Louie. "He needs to come here."

He left, I thought. *Snap out of it.*

"I'm *mungry*," I told Louie. "Let's go eat." I was mad he left and hungry at the same time.

The following day, Tony called for Louie, and of course, I answered the phone. We talked as Louie and Mutsi walked in the door. "Who's on the phone, Sara?"

"Unfortunately, it's for you, Louie."

Later that afternoon as I was scheduling trucks and keeping record of everyone's hours on the job, the door opened. My heart jumped.

"Would you have dinner with me tonight?"

And I thought, *All my life I've been waiting for you. I have dreamed of you. Now it's all come true. I'm so happy that God introduced me to you.*

We started dating while Uncle Tony was in prison, and I was crazy about him. Louie would say to me, "Be careful, babe." And I never knew what he meant by that. When Tony would come into the office, Louie and Mutsi never left my side, and I didn't understand why. I found out later that they were reporting back to Uncle Tony because Uncle Tony didn't want to see me hurt.

We talked, or he talked because I couldn't say much. We went out to dinner together and went to shows. We went to New York to see Engelbert Humperdinck. Every day I loved him more and more. He was so thoughtful and wonderful, and when we weren't together, I missed him so very much. It was like Engelbert sang his songs just for us. "The Very Thought of You." Now I knew what it meant when my girlfriends would tell me how madly in love they were. "I'm living in a kind of daydream, I'm happy as can be." There was nothing like it. I was in heaven. The times we went to the beach for sunset with a bottle of wine, and he would sing to me "Moonlight Becomes You," another one of our Engelbert songs.

"Stop it some more," I would tell him.

Uncle Tony was pissed.

Holy S——t

We dated a lot and started seeing each other every day. I couldn't live without him. Then one night a year later, Tony unexpectedly came over to pick me up, brought a bottle of wine, got our chairs, and we went to the beach for sunset. But he was acting kind of strange, I thought as we sat and opened the wine. I was getting nervous.

"Will you marry me?"

Holy s——t! Say that again. To say I went into shock is putting it lightly. I couldn't speak.

"I guess that's a no. Do you want me to leave?"

Did you ever hear anyone stutter one word, "Yy-ee-ss."

The next day when I told Louie the Killer, he was not happy. That Sunday when I visited Trenton State

Prison and told Uncle Tony, the fit hit the shan. "I'll be out soon," he said, and I didn't understand what he meant.

I told Mom and Dad and my sisters, and now it was time to plan a wedding—my wedding—with the love of my life. And what greater music to have the band play at our wedding than love songs by Engelbert and to have the first dance with my husband to Engelbert's song, "If I Could Love You More." Oh my!

I wanted to wait until Uncle Tony got out of prison, but that wouldn't be for another three years, and so I was given his blessing and told not to wait. We started our list: Tony's mom, sister and her husband, all his relatives, my mom, dad, sisters and their husbands, aunts and uncles, Victor and Armani Hammond with their wives, and of course, Louie the Killer with his wife, Musti and his wife, and all the Wise Guys and their spouses. And, of course, the gang that I grew up with. We had quite a large wedding with everybody singing and dancing. Yes, we had our first dance together as husband and wife, and the band played Engelbert. And my world stood still.

Six Months Later

About six months later, I went to my doctor and confirmed that I was pregnant. Did I tell you yet how happy I was?

That night when Tony came home, I had a special bottle of wine chilled, open, and I was ready for action.

"Is something going on that I should know about?" he asked, sort of like, "Am I in trouble with Uncle Tony?"

"Sweetheart," I said while pouring the wine and playing *The Best of Engelbert*. "I went to the doctor today. We're pregnant." My man was so happy he had tears in his eyes.

The next day, I had to take a special drive to tell Uncle Tony. Although he wasn't happy about the father being Tony, he was very excited to hear the news. "I'll be out soon," he would say, hoping his parole would go through. Every Sunday, he watched me get bigger and bigger. I finally found out the baby was a boy, and the excitement grew as he grew. Uncle Tony would say to me, "When that baby is born, you better take him in here to visit me." And I'd reply, "Uncle Tony, his first trip out of the house will be here to visit you."

Nine months later, I had a rough night, and at six thirty that morning, I called my doctor. I had his personal phone number because my sister and he were friends, and he told me to call him anytime I needed him. Okay, six thirty. I needed him. I said, "Doc, I'm ready."

He replied, "Okay, Sara, I'll meet you at the hospital."

As soon as I hung up, I called my sister, Liz, and told her the same thing. "I am ready."

"Sara," she said. "I'll meet you at the hospital."

Tony, the love of my life, helped me out to the car, and we drove to the hospital and went into the emergency room. Needless to say, the emergency room was full of sick people, some worse off than the others, but I knew it was only a matter of minutes when my precious baby would be born, so they better get me in there fast or I'd deliver right here.

When my doctor came in, he examined me, and by this time, my sister arrived. Boy, was I happy to see her. "Sara." he said. "You're not ready yet."

"Don't tell me. I'm ready. I want to get this over with!" said bright, intelligent me. "I've had enough. I'm ready."

"Tell you what I'll do, I'll put you in a room for a while, and we'll keep our eyes on you." So my sister, thank God, stayed with me while I waited patiently for the doctor to admit me.

My sister got a wheelchair and took me up to my room. "Sara," she said. "Don't be too disappointed if the baby isn't born today."

"I'm ready."

In the meantime, I heard screams from the next room. "He's never going to screw me again!" A minute later, I heard, "I'll kill the bastard if he tries to come near me again!" Oh, hell. I need to pee.

Once in the bathroom, an amazingly horrible thing happened. I had a miscarriage. How did this happen? It couldn't be! I came out of the bathroom crying hysterically. "Liz!" I called my sister. "This can't be happening!"

And my patient, beautiful sister ran to me. "What's the matter, Sara? What happened?"

"I had a miscarriage! I'm all wet. I went to the bathroom and had a miscarriage!"

I think the nurses had an uproar laughing at me. "Sara," my sister said. "Your water broke. You're ready to deliver."

"I told you I was ready! Get the doctor. Get the nurse. Get me outta here!"

Now I could understand why the girl was screaming that he was never going to get near her again.

And then my whole life changed. My baby boy was born, and it was the most precious moment of my life. It didn't matter that I had turned into a killer; it didn't matter that I was working with Uncle Tony. The pain of delivery didn't even matter. One look at my baby, and nothing else mattered. Nobody was going to take him from me. Ever.

"Sis, you got him?" said intelligent me. "I got him," she said. "Hold him until he gets his name bracelet." *I don't want any mistakes made and babies switched*, I thought. *My temper might rise, watch out.* I passed out.

That afternoon, I was so hungry because I had nothing to eat. My husband was there and asked, "Sara, are you hungry?"

Am I hungry? "I'd kill for a cup of tea and some toast," was what I told him. As my mom, dad, and sisters came to visit me, Tony went out to get my tea and toast. Little did I know he was going to be gone for hours, and when he finally came back, he had a Coke and a steak sandwich with hot pepper. Figure that one out.

Life was good. My husband and my baby, Joey, meant everything to me. We named him after his grandfather, my husband's father. I wasn't going into the office for a while so I could stay home and take care of my son. It was the most exciting time of my life. Each day I loved him more and more. I thought of the poem by Victor Hugo: "A mother's arms are made of tenderness, and children sleep soundly in them."

The time finally came…it was time to take my son out of the house. Excitement. I gave him a bath and was dressing him when my husband walked in. "Oh, where are we going?"

"We can go out when I get back," I said.

"Oh, no," he said.

"Oh, yes," I said. "When we get home, I'll go anywhere you want to go. In the meantime, the car should be here soon." No sooner did I say that when the car pulled up, so I wrapped my baby up, went out to the car, and off we went to Trenton State Prison for my baby's first day out of the house.

It took about an hour to drive to Trenton as usual, and when we pulled in, we had no parking problems. Of course, my driver took us to the front door, helped us out of the car, and waited outside for us. There was no way he wanted to go inside.

When I checked in and went inside, I saw one of the inmates I knew from Peterstown or the Burg—Anthony or Fat Anthony as everyone called him. He was sweeping the floor, and as soon as he saw me, he came over to see my baby boy. Apparently, he knew I was coming. Then Injun, a friend of Uncle Tony's, saw us and came over to say hello. It was like old home week in Trenton State Prison. Finally, they brought Uncle Tony out.

Uncle Tony picked up his phone, I picked up my phone, and he was so happy to see us. There were tears in his eyes as he said, "I didn't really think you would bring Baby Joey in to see me."

I promised him we would stay very close and that there was nothing that would separate us.

"Now, get the hell out of this place, Unk. We need you home." I could see he was holding back tears. I know my uncle.

4

Farm Life

"Let's buy a farm! We can have horses, cows, raise our own food, fresh milk, and eggs. What do you say?"

"Are you crazy? We don't know anything about farming," I said.

"Let's just look."

Pittstown, New Jersey, here we come, I thought. Forty acres in the middle of nowhere. "Mom, can I have a pony?"

"But of course."

"Mom, can I have baby chicks?"

"Of course."

Now I don't know if you know anything about baby chicks, but I ordered them fifty at a time to raise for food in the chicken coop. "Mom, can I keep one as a pet?"

"Of course. Tell you what. You pick one, you name it. We'll keep it separate so we know it's yours, and the rest we'll raise for food." And so Henny was chosen.

We then got a couple of horses and two ponies—one for my son, Joey, and one for his cousin, Dominick, who would spend weekends with us, and they named them Patches and Pipsqueak. During the week when Joey would come home from kindergarten, I would take my horse, and he would jump on Pipsqueak, and we'd ride to the mailbox to get our mail, then he would run out to the chicken coop to play with Henny. Well, as Henny grew and grew, we were quite surprised to discover that Henny turned out to be a rooster.

One day after playing in the chicken coop with Henny, Joey came in the house, and his face was bleeding under his eye, and I said, "Sweetheart, what happened?"

"Oh, Mom, Henny did that."

Like a good mother, I didn't say anything. I just got him cleaned up, and we played inside until Daddy came home. When Daddy came home from work, Joey explained to him what happened with Henny.

Like a good mother, the following day when Joey went to school, I took that sucker Henny and had Danny, a worker who was living with us, wring his neck. I cleaned him up and made a big pot of chicken soup. When Joey came home from school and he went to the chicken coop, he came running back inside the house, "Mom, I can't find Henny!"

"Oh, sweetheart, you know, it's mating season. Maybe Henny flew the coop to find a mate, and he'll be back soon. But sit down and have some chicken soup I made for you. It's cold outside."

"Oh, Mom, this soup is so good."

Didn't tell him anything!

*   *   *

My sister, Gina, who is Dominick's mother, came to the farm one weekend and just had to tell me what she did, but she waited until nobody else could hear.

"I tried to kill my husband," she told me in confidence.

I thought, could murder in a family be hereditary?

"What happened?" I asked.

"Well, I knew he was cheating on me because his girlfriend called. She was trying to get me to leave him."

"And so what did you do? Did you get hurt, Gina?"

"No, I didn't get hurt, but when he came home, he had been drinking so much that he fell asleep in the chair, so I put a plastic bag around his head, hoping it would suffocate him, and then I could just take it off. But he was breathing so hard, and the plastic bag just kept going in and out, in and out."

"And what did you do?" I asked.

"I put an elastic band around it. I figured he was still getting air, and I needed to stop the air from getting in. But then he started coughing, and I got scared, so I took it off. And then he woke up and went to bed. When he woke up the next morning, he saw a red ring around his neck and asked what happened to him, and I told him I didn't know, that maybe somebody tried to kill him."

We really laughed at that one.

And so as the months passed, I would bring Joey into the office with Louie the Killer and Mutsi. The drive wasn't that far from the farm. After two years, Uncle Tony was released and was coming home. Happiness. It was time to leave the office and turn it back into their hands to run. What a nice feeling, my job was done.

We then got on a schedule of every Friday night meeting Uncle Tony at a restaurant called The Paddock down the Jersey Shore. My husband was even invited, and as I found out later, he was invited so Uncle Tony and Louie could reaffirm with him that he better behave himself, or else. I didn't know that my husband had a reputation for being a "ladies' man," and this was their way of keeping him under control.

The Paddock was a quaint restaurant, and Uncle Tony knew the owner, so we always had our own private room. There were always about twelve people that met for our Friday night dinners, and we had our so-called assigned seats. Of course, Uncle Tony was at the head of the table, I sat to his right, and Joey sat between us. My husband was down at the other end—way down at the other end—but he understood this was the only day of the week I saw my uncle and my friends from the office.

One night, I dressed Joey up in his blue denim pants, blue shirt, and blue suede shoes. He looked so cute. When we walked in The Paddock, Bobby B. was sitting in my seat. I walked in and said, "That's okay, Unk. I'll sit down at the other end."

He didn't say a word but just looked at Bobby, and you know what they say. If looks could kill…well, Bobby tried to get out of his seat so fast that the chair went tumbling over, and he went flying. I laughed.

As we sat and talked, Uncle Tony started teasing Joey, and Joey was getting like—you know how little kids can act when they get teased—and I'd say, "Joseph, mind your manners." And Uncle Tony would tease, and I'd say, "Joseph, mind your manners." But Uncle Tony took it too far and continued to tease, and then Joey turned around and punched him in the nose!

"Joseph!"

"That's okay. I wanted to see how long I could tease him."

"Well, then, you deserved it," said intelligent me.

The time came when I confided to Uncle Tony about my kill and how I went to South America to get away and then to Europe and Morocco and how I was afraid to come home. I knew my secret was safe with him. After all, I had never told anyone about this before except the Del Ray Debs. We talked and talked, and he reassured me that if I was ever caught, he would do everything he could to help me.

"But if you want to make some money, I have a job for you."

"What kind of a job, Unk?"

"Bobby Genovese has gotten out of hand. I'm afraid he has to go. Would you be interested in doing a hit?"

"Bobby Genovese?"

"Bobby has been stealing from us and starting a lot of trouble. I tried talking to him, but he just won't listen. Nobody would suspect you, and I'll make it worth your while. You'd be perfect for the job. He'll never suspect it from you."

Well, Bobby Genovese and I were a "thing" while we were growing up and in school, and our parents always thought we would marry, but I wasn't crazy about him. Oh, well.

The deal sounded interesting. "And I'll give you forty thousand dollars." Boy, my Uncle Tony was the best.

"Deal."

Well, I figure I need a little help on planning this whole thing, and I know my friend, Chaz (who I used to beat up all the time), has a lot of experience in this field by this time. But I know Chaz is on trial in New Jersey for a crime he didn't commit, of course, but I'll seek him out anyway.

"*Princesa*," he called me. "What's going on? They're killing me over here. I got word that during the trial tomorrow, they're going to arrest me for murder. The next time we see each other, we could be seventy years old."

My poor baby, I thought. "Chaz," I said. "I don't know about you, but if it was me, I'd take off. I wouldn't go to my trial tomorrow knowing that I'd be arrested and booked for murder."

He kind of thought about it, and then he said, "And where would you go?" I told him, and he said, "Would you pick up my son and have him at your house tonight at midnight, and I'll come over? I want him to hear it from me and nobody else."

"Sure," said happy-to-oblige me. "It will be my pleasure."

So I called his son, went to pick him up, and at midnight Chaz came over to talk to—let's just call him Pablo, as in Pablo Diego Picasso if I'm Sara Bocelli. So Pablo came over, Chaz came over, and he told him, "Pablo, when I was out last Halloween, I had dinner with this guy at the Holiday Inn and afterward took him out in the parking lot and killed him. I had to do it because he was a squealer, and everybody would be going to prison if we didn't get rid of him. I wanted you to hear it from me first."

"Chaz, you were out on Halloween, killed somebody, and you didn't even wear a costume so nobody could recognize you?" *Dummy*, I thought. *I'm not going to get advice from him about Bobby.*

So the next day, I read in the newspaper that Chaz was a no-show at his trial. After that, the news was that he was tried in absentia and convicted. They were looking for him.

As the world turned or the years passed, there was no word from Chaz until about three years later when I get a phone call. "*Princesa*, they're closing in on me."

I said, "Where in the world are you?"

Chaz said, "I'm right where you told me to go, but I'm going to turn myself in. I feel like they're closing in on me." Needless to say, Chaz was in prison for many, many years after that, but I went to visit him also. I'm just a good-hearted Peterstown girl.

Getting back to Bobby Genovese, I needed a plan, a plan that would work, and I couldn't wait until Halloween to dress in a costume to collect my forty thousand dollars from Uncle Tony. I wanted it now, so I needed a plan. *Do I take him out in broad daylight? Do I do it at his home? Do I do it in the car? Or do we go away, perhaps camping? My husband will understand if I'm gone for a few hours. Let me figure this one out. Most of his neighbors know me, so I can't go there. But who wants to be in the car with him alone, or go camping with him?* I thought of something Oscar Wilde had said, "Always forgive your enemies. Nothing annoys them so much."

No, I need an exquisite plan. I need to get on the inside of his mind while staying on the outside so I'm not suspected. Bobby, Bobby, Bobby, you're taking me away from my son and my wonderful husband. I need to do this soon because the more I think about it, the more you're going to suffer. I'll start with finding out where he goes at night.

My Exquisite Plan

I went to the store and purchased a blond wig, large glasses, and a pair of gloves and stuffed a pants suit I had so I looked heavier than I was. Nobody should be able to recognize me or pick me out in a photo lineup.

That night, Bobby went to pick up his date, and little did he know that I was right behind him following him. Ugly girl.

"Bobby, Bobby," I said to myself. "You act like a normal person, but you're not." I followed them to an Italian restaurant downtown New York, where I waited outside in my car, and with every minute he made me wait, I got angrier and angrier. "This bastard is going to pay for keeping me away from my son and husband."

It was a quaint little Italian restaurant, you know, the ones with the checked green and white tablecloths, candles on the tables, dim lighting. It didn't have another room with a bar, but they did serve beer and wine. As I peeked in the window of the restaurant, I could see they had a bottle of red wine on the table, and they were laughing at who knows what while his hands were all over her. I watched as they ate what looked like Fettuccine Alfredo. It was making me hungry. More wine, more laughing. I was getting annoyed and cold. The night was chilly, and I wanted to be home in the warmth of my own home.

I went back to my car to wait as the night progressed, thinking this was never going to end. When they finally left the restaurant, I followed them to her house where he parked the car, and they disappeared inside for about an hour. He then came out, returned to his car, and drove home.

The following night, it was the same thing with a different girl. He picked her up, but this time they went to a fancy restaurant in Little Italy downtown New York. He must have liked this one. This girl was prettier, so I guess he wanted to show her off to his friends. She was a redhead with a slender figure and high heels on. You could see she was crazy about him.

He parked the car, went around to her side, opened the door for her, and together they went inside the restaurant. I waited a while, and then I got out of my car and walked over to the restaurant to peek in the window to see what was going on. This restaurant had a big beautiful bar and served alcohol, and their tablecloths were elite and smart-looking. There were beautifully lit candles on each table, and I could see they had a basket of Italian bread on their table. Once again, Bobby ordered red wine, but I knew he liked drinking red wine from our time dating each other, even in high school. I watched them for a while as they ate dinner, drank their wine, laughing. As usual, his hands were all over her. *Bobby, Bobby, Bobby, you're going to pay for this.* I had no compassion.

Eventually, their damn dinner was over. *It's about time*, I thought, as my temper rose. When they came out of the restaurant, I knew exactly what Bobby, Bobby, Bobby was up to, so I had a plan to outsmart him. This was now officially outstanding!

When they finally pulled away, I got out of my car, locked it, and went into the same restaurant. I sat at their table before the waiter had a chance to clean it off, and I ordered a drink. I knew Bobby would be at this girl's home for at least an hour, and I had time to waste before my plan went into action.

As I sat and ordered my drink, I unobtrusively looked at the tablecloth before they cleared it away. Then I said to the waiter, "No need to hurry. Take your time." I was up to no good, and the waiter was enabling my bad behavior. I needed to find something I could use later.

And as I used my large menu as a shield, I found what I was looking for: a strand of long red hair. Nothing like working in an attorney's office to pick up hints like this. I sat back and took out the small plastic envelope I brilliantly brought with me for situations such as this, and I picked up the strand of hair, put it in the envelope, sealed it, and put it away for my *magnevil* plan. Yes, you heard that right. Magnevil. My magnificently evil plan!

By this time, I was hungry and was also happy because my plan was now taking shape. I thought, there's faith and hope, and if all else fails, there's pizza. Besides, I had to waste an hour because I knew where Bobby was going and what he was going to do.

"May I take your order?" said the waiter as he brought my wine.

Oh, yes, you adorable guy. You may take my order all day long, I thought.

I knew Bobby wouldn't be home right away, so I ate my pizza and drank my wine. When I was finished, with my strands of red evidence tucked away, I left the restaurant milling over my outstanding plan of action, thinking I'd be home soon. I had to be very careful about the rest of my night. Every step I made, every move I made had to be without a trace. I could do this. I *had* to do this.

I got in my car and drove close to a subway station that I knew had trains to Bobby's house, and I parked my car on the street because I knew it would be safe until I got back, and I did not want my car seen in Bobby's neighborhood. Still with my blond wig on, I got out of my car, looking around to be sure I was not attracting attention and nobody would recognize me. I went down to the subway, bought a ticket from the machine with cash, and took the train to Bobby's house because I knew he wouldn't be back home yet. At this hour, there weren't many people on the train, so I felt safe, except for the two guys with tattoos. They had a teardrop under one eye, and you know what that stands for. Well, at least, it was only one teardrop, which means one kill. Perhaps I should get a teardrop tattoo. No, forget about it.

Smart Asses

It seemed to me they were in their early twenties, rough-looking. They both had pants down below their waist, and I figured if I had to I could pull their pants down and run like hell, but where would the fun in that be? They had sweatshirts on with hoods up and were looking me over. As one "gentleman" looked at me,

I could see his mind beginning to wander, just as the prince had done. They looked at each other and mumbled something and then looked at me and laughed. Oh, this is going to be fun. I just wish it isn't now at a time when I'm so close to forty thousand dollars and making Uncle Tony proud of me.

As one of them had his eyes on me, he started to approach, and I thought, *Here we go. I better be prepared.* So I put one hand in my pocket and grabbed a hold of my killer knife, and he said, "What's up, baby? Where you goin'? Wanna come home with me?"

With that, I quickly took my hand out of my pocket and, with a smile on my face, put my arm around him and held the tip of my knife to his neck and said, "Well, sweetheart, I don't think tonight's the night for us. Now at the next stop, you little boys can get off the train so we don't have any misunderstanding. *Capisce, gidrul?*"

My Italian was coming in handy. I didn't even curse, which is saying something since incidentally aside from the words *capisce* and *gidrul*, the only other Italian I remember are curse words. I kept my knife at the vein on his neck until the train stopped, and his friend ran off and he followed. "That girl is crazy, man," I could hear them say as they ran for cover.

I took the train to Bobby's stop, got out, and walked to his place, not looking at anyone along the way and keeping to myself. *If I see anybody I know, I'll have to abort and try another time*, I thought. *Keep to the plan. Make Uncle Tony proud. Collect your forty thousand dollars. Go home and raise your son.*

I got to Bobby's house, walked around to the back where nobody would see me and with my gloves on so I left no fingerprints, I took my tool out to unlock the back door. By this time, I had worked up a sweat and was getting nervous and a bit scared. What if I can't do it? What if he takes my gun and shoots me? What would happen to my son? What would my husband think? All these thoughts were going through my head when I heard the front door unlock and Bobby was coming in.

I was by the back door, so I quickly made my way into his bedroom...quietly. *Can I do this? Will I do this?* I hid silently, holding my breath at times for fear of being discovered. When I heard him finally go into the bathroom and put the shower on, I came out of hiding. By this time, I was into it and ready to go. My courage was stimulating me.

I walked into his bathroom and opened the shower curtain as quickly as I could and saw the surprise in his eyes. "Bobby, Bobby, Bobby, my love. Come to me." As I saw an expression of happiness and confusion, I made it a point to confuse him and instill fear. I wanted his fear, I needed his fear. His fear was stimulating to me. Where did I come from?

I took Bobby by the hand and guided him out of his shower and into his bedroom. The stupid thing didn't even ask how I got in his house and what was I doing there. He followed my directions and listened to everything I told him. As I brought him to his bed, I whispered in his ear, "Bobby, let's play a game." I took off my clothes, and he got excited. I handcuffed him to his bed, and he was aroused by my taking charge. "Let me take you to another world, a world of pleasure and happiness." What do they call that, erotica sex, or something like that? You can find that on the Internet.

As I proceeded to tie his belt around his neck and start pressure, I could see the confused look in his eyes. He couldn't do anything because the stupid motherf——r let me handcuff him to the bed. I danced over to his shoes and gently took a shoelace off one of his shoes and gently, ever so gently, danced back to him and put it around his neck with the belt, all with a smile on my face. I thought, *Let's not let a little thing like murder get in the way of us having a good time.*

"Sara, what are you doing?"

"I'm sorry if I insinuated, Bobby. I meant to be very clear." There was a second of happiness and then surprise and then shock and fear as I pulled the belt and shoelace tighter and tighter.

He gagged, he choked, and he tried to scream for help, but it was all to no avail. I was in charge. I was in control. *Oh, Bobby, this is for all the times you cheated on me in high school. This is for all the money you stole from Uncle Tony*, I thought as I pulled the belt and shoelace tighter and tighter. I wanted revenge. I pulled and pulled.

As he fought and tried to get free of the handcuffs, he got weaker and weaker, and I was happy. I was in control. I never felt so much power. This was me. This was me in power. I wanted this power. He fought, but there was nothing he could do. I was in control. I put fear in his eyes. It was me that had him handcuffed and sweating.

As he fought and fought and tried to scream for help, nothing came out. Bobby took his last breath, and I looked him in the eyes and said, "All Is Forgiven."

I took a deep breath. Inhale. Exhale. Smile. My work was almost done.

As I stood up and got dressed, I was careful not to touch anything, but I still had on my fancy gloves for double protection of fingerprints. After I was dressed, I checked to be sure there was none of my hair on the sheets and then went in my purse, took out my little plastic envelope, and laid the strand of red hair on the pillow next to Bobby, Bobby, Bobby's head. I wondered who would be blamed for this. Not me, for sure. Uncle Tony will be proud of me.

I left the house the same way that I entered—through the back door—with my wig and gloves on, careful not to be seen. I had mixed feelings. I was overjoyed thinking of my cash, but the look in Bobby's eyes as he was fading at my hands was somewhat overpowering. I quickly walked to the subway station, keeping my eyes down to be sure no one looked at me directly, and also to be sure my wig stayed on. I didn't want the wind to blow it away. Wish I brought the wine with me. I got to the subway station, purchased my one-way ticket at the machine again with cash instead of purchasing it at a booth with a human so I was not recognized, and went to my platform to wait for the oncoming train that would take me to my car and eventually home. My work was done.

I drove home, and as I reached the house, I thought, *There's no place like home.* I opened the garage door with my little gadget, drove in, and parked. I got out of the car and felt exhaustion set in. I sure did have a couple of rough days and was happy it was over with.

"Have a nice day?" said Tony. *Huh?* I thought. *He must know.*

"Yes, I had a pleasant day. Nothing out of the ordinary," said little ole' liar me. After all, I didn't want him to know because the less he knew, the better off he was.

Not like the time he was in cahoots with the guys making counterfeit twenty-dollar bills and told me about it. And then when the FBI came to our house with a search warrant, they handcuffed him and sat him down in the living room while they searched the house. Poor little Joey was an infant, and I asked the FBI agent, "Do you mind if I take the baby in the back to change his diaper?"

"No, that's okay." That was awfully nice of the schmuck. So I took Joey into the bedroom and packed his diaper with the counterfeit bills, wrapped him in a blanket, and took him in the living room. I then asked the FBI agent if Tony's daughter, who also lived with us, could take the baby outside for a walk and away from the commotion. "Sure," he replied.

But I had to think quickly about that one. I couldn't communicate to my husband what I was doing because I didn't want to be caught, so he sat there handcuffed, sweating, not knowing what was going on and thinking the FBI was going to find the counterfeit twenties and haul him off to jail, and then he was surprised as hell that they didn't find anything.

Anyhow, when I got home after the Bobby Genovese night, I told my husband that nothing was new and went into Joey's room to give him a kiss good night. Poor baby was sound asleep. He was so adorable, and I loved him with all my heart. Was there any way I could get caught and have to go through a murder trial? Would my husband stand by me if that did happen, or would he try to take my son away?

So many thoughts were going through my head when I heard a sound and got scared. I turned my head to see what it was, and there was Tony standing there. Would he ever do such a thing to me? I wondered. Instead, we sat on the bed together admiring our baby boy. But my baby looked like me, not his father.

"Let's go to sleep," I said. As we went into the bedroom, I put on my favorite Engelbert CD and then fell asleep in my husband's arms to the song, "You'll Never Know." I thought of the lyrics, *If there is some other way to prove that I love you, I swear I don't know how. You'll never know if you don't know now.* In the words of Pablo Neruda, we were "so intimate that when he falls asleep, my eyes close."

5

Job Well Done

The next day when I woke up, it was just like any other day. I put the coffee on, made my husband breakfast as usual, and waited for Joey to get up to spend the day with him.

"I think I'll take Joey down to see Uncle Tony today," I said as he was eating his breakfast. "We'll see you tonight for dinner, or do you want to meet us down there and we'll all have dinner together?"

He was still somewhat intimidated by the guys because when he was in their presence, they never took their eyes off of him.

"No, that's okay. I'll meet you back here."

I never told my husband, Tony, about my night before because I didn't want to worry him, but I couldn't wait until he left so Joey and I could go down to Uncle Tony's to tell him the good news. Maybe I'll get two teardrop tattoos. I don't think so.

The drive down to the Jersey Shore was uneventful. I parked the car, and Joey and I went into the office where Uncle Tony, Louie, and Mutsi were waiting for me. Nothing was said when I walked in, but they each came up and gave me a long hug. I felt important. Uncle Tony took my hand and then Joey's, and we went into his private office and shut the door. These were unspoken times. You never knew if there was a bug somewhere, but he went into his safe, took out the cash, and gave me fifty thousand dollars.

"No, we agreed on forty thousand dollars. Here's ten back," I said.

"The ten is for the red strand of hair. It's all over the news that they found red hair on his pillow, and they were testing it. Thank you very much," he said, and that was the last I heard of it.

Apparently, the girl didn't have a record, so they had no DNA on her, and they had no other clues. Unsolved murder mystery. All was good.

We all went out for lunch to celebrate and, of course, play with my adorable little boy, with Uncle Tony teasing as usual. But Joey got tough, and I didn't restrict him from hitting anyone if they deserved it.

"Do you want to call your husband to drive down and we can all have dinner together?"

"Thank you, Unk, but not tonight. We'll see you on Friday."

We took the hour-long drive home and stopped to pick up some red wine along the way because I was making a special dinner tonight. I'm not stressed anymore from thinking about how to kill Bobby, and I want a nice quiet evening at home with my husband, listening to Engelbert's song, "A Lovely Way to Spend an Evening," and his CD *You Belong To My Heart*.

I went home, made dinner, and sang. I gave my son an early dinner and put him to bed. It was seven o'clock, but where was Tony? When the telephone rang, Tony's voice came on the line, and he said, "I'm sorry I won't be home for dinner tonight. Something came up. I'll see you later." *Oh, damn*, I thought. *This isn't such a lovely way to spend an evening. It must be important.*

Within the next few weeks, things remained the same at home, and I would occasionally bring my son to the office to see everybody. On the days I didn't go down to Long Branch, I took Joey into New York to see Uncle Victor at the gallery. We would have fun with Uncle Victor either by taking him to the gallery or sometimes by taking a horse and carriage around Central Park or by going to Rockefeller Center. Joey loved walking around New York City.

Or I would tell Joey the story about Aunt Jenny and Uncle Skippy and little, red Fiat convertible that I bought when I traded in my Studebaker. "My Fiat was so small that when Uncle Skippy sat in the front seat, I had to cover Aunt Jenny with olive oil so I could slide her in the backseat of the car," I'd say, and he would laugh and laugh.

Well, I didn't have any more calls to do that thing I don't want to speak about right now...you know, that Bobby Genovese thing...but I was glad I could be of help. I didn't hear anything more on that or the prince. It seems they didn't have enough proof or evidence to charge, or even investigate anybody. But every time I think of the prince and how stupid I was, I want to kill him again.

"Birthday party time. Joey's going to be five years old. Let's plan a party." With that, I called our unorganized gang and planned the party in two weeks downstairs in our recreation room. We had a complete kitchen downstairs and a bar, so it was easy to plan. I cooked meatballs, sausage, chicken parmesan, macaroni, and Italian bread for a week. We stocked the bar and hired a local country band that came in Saturday night. We just rocked the house. Work like you don't need money, love like you've never been hurt, and dance like no one's watching. My friend Frank from Caracas was in town, and he joined us and said, "You're a party animal."

Sunday was a day of rest. On Monday, Victor called. "Do you want to take Joey to New York tomorrow and we'll have a birthday party for him at the gallery?"

"Sure, Victor." I thought as long as no one was looking for the prince's killer, we would be okay. A party at the gallery, Joey would love that. I remember one day Victor took us upstairs to his private office where there was one wall of curtains. He opened the curtains, and—wow!—there was a beautiful Pablo Picasso original painting worth millions of dollars.

As the world turned, I got home one afternoon, and my husband was there with some of the guys. "Hi. Everything okay?" I asked him. With that, he showed

me what were some legal papers, a subpoena to appear.
I could recognize the papers from working at the lawyer's office.

"I was indicted under the RICO statute," he said. "I
have to call the lawyer and turn myself in tomorrow. The
prosecuting attorney signed his name to the documents.
An Italian guy."

*Why would an Italian man go after Italians and try to
put them in jail? Can't he make a name for himself going
after the criminals and not the unorganized, unwise guys?* I
thought; I didn't want to say it out loud.

Well, he turned himself in, and he pleaded not guilty.
We went through a federal trial and lost, so now my
wonderful husband had to go to prison in Allenwood,
Pennsylvania, for three years. My son would grow these
years without his father, and I must say, my husband,
Tony, was such a good father. That meant selling the
farm and moving back to civilization to be near family
and friends. We sold our forty acres and bought a house
down the Jersey Shore, Point Pleasant, which was closer
to Uncle Tony and Louie.

Over the next few years, I would pack Joey's stuff,
and we would drive to Allenwood to see his dad,

and at night, I would play "Unchained Melody" by Engelbert. "Time goes by so slowly…God speed your love to me."

Joey was growing up. He had been wrestling with his cousins, Johnny and Little Augie, since he was three years old, and he now joined a wrestling team for kids. His dad was still in Allenwood, and one day while I was out, I happened to run into Larry, a friend of mine from school, and we got to talking. It turned out Larry went into professional wrestling, you know, those hulky guys on TV. I took the boys—my son and nephews—to watch him wrestle at his next match, and then we all went back to my house to watch them—the wrestlers, their kids whom they had at the matches, and referees—on TV. Strange, right?

Another friend played football with the Jets, and then after he retired from football, he started working in Atlantic City in one of the casinos, bringing in football players and coaches to the casino. He was also in charge of boxing. So of course, I would bring Joey to Atlantic City on weekends when there was a big fight because we had free tickets and a free room for the night. But I was a good wife. I still adored my husband and couldn't wait for him to come home to us.

Finally, the day came when Tony was coming home from prison. "Joey, we're going to pick up Daddy tomorrow. He's coming home," I said, and he jumped for joy. He was now eight years old and looking forward to this day. We got up early the next morning, drove to Allenwood to pick Daddy up, and turned around and drove home. Mutsi came with us to help with the driving. By the time we got home, it was late. Joey was tired, so he said good night to Mom and Dad.

Yes, it was different having my husband all to myself again. I had a bottle of champagne chilled, and of course we had to play an Engelbert CD and spend the night in each other's arms. It was so wonderful to have him home with us. Simply wonderful, and I thought the first duty of love is to listen, and I vowed to listen. Not to obey but to listen.

That Saturday evening, I planned a welcome home party for him. We decorated, I bought wine and champagne, and my whole family helped me cook. I made a big pot of gravy and meatballs, sausage, lasagna, a big antipasto. Injun, who had been in Allenwood with Uncle Tony but was released about the same time, brought over lobsters because he was out lobstering. We had a band in the backyard. We had our lives back. Our families came over, lots and lots of friends, girlfriends, and guy friends—the wrestler and ex-football player.

Did I say girlfriends? There was one in particular who I noticed kept eyeing up Tony, but I didn't think anything of it. I knew he wouldn't stray, and neither would I. And my friends Geoff and Fay surprised us and also came to the party. I hadn't seen them in a long time.

As the years passed, I didn't get any calls on that Bobby Genovese thing or the prince, but I kept busy with all that was going on in my family, especially with my crazy sisters, and my friends, and I took cake decorating classes to divert my attention.

After things settled down somewhat, Tony was going out to work during the day, while Joey was in school. He was growing up to be such a wonderful kid. I was so proud of him and loved him with all my heart—well, I still love him; I shouldn't say "loved." By this time, he was in middle school and had a school project that he was working on. "Mom, I'd like you to read this before I hand it in tomorrow, and tell me if you see any spelling errors."

I read:

The Things that Make America Great

The most wonderful quality that America has to offer its people is freedom. This quality is what makes America a great country. Freedom comes in many forms, like free enterprise, Welfare, Wall Street, World Services, and Social Security are on the social society side. Another form of freedom is competition, like the Olympics, and don't forget Bob Hope and apple pie. One thing that we have and the Russians don't is equality. One other great thing about America is the Bill of Rights.

My son goes on to describe the Bill of Rights, the Amendments to the Constitution, the Presidents of the United States, starting with George Washington; he goes on to describe memorable happenings in American history, and ends his paper with:

Be Proud to Be American!

My little boy is growing up.

"Joseph, this paper is fantastic. I'm very proud of you."

He was so busy with school and cousins and friends that I got to thinking, *I need something to do.* I went to the school wrestling matches that he was in and also to the baseball games he played in, but I needed something to do or I was going to get in trouble. I was always raised by my parents to stay away from court, but I said to myself, *I always wanted to be a court reporter. Why not now? And this is something Joey would be proud of me for.*

Everybody tried to talk me out of it, but I knew they made good money, and it was exciting, and that was what I wanted to do. I didn't want to stay at home every day and watch TV. So I searched the court reporting schools, and I found one not far from home. I called and made an appointment, and went in.

"This is a course where you go at your own pace," the director told me. "And you have to take English, medical, and legal terminology besides learning the language of the machine and building your speed to two hundred twenty-five words a minute just to get out of school."

"But I already know English," I responded.

"Yes, but it's mandatory."

Can I do that? Hell, yes.

So every morning, when Joey would go to school and my husband went to work, I went to school. We started with fifty-five people in my class. Madonna Mia, I can do this. First class we started learning the alphabet. "I friggin' know the alphabet," I wanted to say, but guess what? I didn't know *their* alphabet. It seems my alphabet and theirs was not the same. *What the hell is this?* Totally confused, I went to my second class: Medical. "What the hell is this? I'm not going to be a doctor."

Still oppressively stressed from my alphabet class, medical class, and the machine, I then went on to my next class: Legal Terminology. I want to kill myself. "The H-R on your left hand is the combination for the letter L."

"Shut up. I heard you twice the first time," I wanted to tell her.

By the time I left school on my first day, I thought to myself, *This course is brutal, cruel, inhuman, and painful.*

When I got home, my husband said to me, "How was your class today?"

I said, "No sweat. I can do it." Was I a good liar or what? *How in the world am I going to do this?* I thought.

Well, our court reporting class through the months dwindled down. I never was so confused in my life. I never misunderstood something so much. I would walk out of there, saying, what the hell did I just experience?

But I was too darned hardheaded to quit. I thought of my instructor's words, "Don't dwell on stupidity. Education is the spice of life." So I practiced and practiced and didn't know what the hell I was doing. English? I thought I knew the English language. Every word somebody says you have to write, so what? Words that aren't even in the dictionary you have to write. Why can't I just write what I think they're saying instead? Once my instructor said to us, "We're going to take down testimony in Spanish." Shhhiiittt!

Two years later when I graduated, there were three of us. *Okay, now what?* I thought. *Now what do I do? I'm a court reporter. I know English, I know medical and legal terminology, so what? Should I look for a job?* You bet your ass...after this torture, as I thought of my instructor, "education opens your eyes."

So I started with a company doing depositions. Apparently, you had to have experience before you worked in court, which is really why I went into this. In my devious mind, I wanted to get all the information I could to help any of Uncle Tony's guys if they got in trouble. Ha! Now we're moving.

6

Party Time

"Tony, let's have a party to celebrate." I called Uncle Tony, Louie, Mutsi, Injun. "Saturday night we're having a party to celebrate my new job as a court reporter."

I invited Mom, Dad, crazy sisters, niece Sandy, nephews Salvatore, Little Augie, Nicky, Danny—basically the whole crew. I wanted to party. I called some of my girlfriends, he called some of the guys, and we had a party. One of my girlfriends even flew in from Florida for the party and stayed at our house. My closest Del Ray Debs girlfriend, Cindy, whom I knew from kindergarten, came over and helped me set things up. When she came in, we looked at each other, but the prince was never mentioned.

Saturday night was the biggest party. There was booze, food—more booze and more food. I even baked a three-tier cake and decorated it. We had fun. We ate, drank, and were merry. The next day, Sunday, was recuperation day. My friend from Florida was staying a few more days with me, and we had a lot to talk about—about all the guys, what was going on with who, and more.

No More Celebration

The next morning, Monday, I got up and saw Tony wasn't in bed; he had apparently gotten up early. So I was on my way into the kitchen when I turned the corner to walk in the doorway to the kitchen and saw Tony and my girlfriend from Florida—let's call her Shitface— they were in an embrace and kissing.

I froze. I couldn't speak. I couldn't move. If someone had come to me and said, "I saw your husband kill somebody in broad daylight," I would have said to them, "Yep, that's him, all right." But if someone had come to me and said, "I saw your husband with another woman," I would have said, "No, you're mistaken. It's not my husband." So when I say I was in shock, I think my heart stopped for at least ten minutes.

With that, he didn't even see me. He walked out the door to go to work. I was standing there still in shock, and Shitface saw me. She was looking at me. Our eyes met, and I couldn't look away. I knew I couldn't kill her now because everybody knew she was here. She got to her feet, but she ran out of the house, never to be seen again. I'm sure she called *him*. When I could get my heart to work again and she was gone, I called him and said quietly and calmly, "If I were you, I would not come home." That was the last I saw of my handsome, wonderful husband for quite some time. He never came home again, and I thought of the song by Paul Anka, "When Somebody Leaves You, That's the Time to Cry."

I had to tell Uncle Tony and Uncle John, and when I did, they were just as quiet and calm as I was. See where I got it from. Disaster. "Stay calm. Be reasonable." I thought of what the Spanish philosopher, Baltasar Gracian, had said: "A wise man (or woman) gets more use from his enemies than a fool from his friends," but there was no way I could forgive this heartache.

I thought of the incinerator in Uncle Tony's house, and because I could see it in Uncle Tony and Uncle John's eyes, I said, "Please. It's my son's father." And I'm sure that was what saved his life. How do you forgive this? I thought we were invincible.

My heart was broken. I thought of the poem by Edgar Allan Poe, "Years of love have been forgot in the hatred of a minute." I cried myself to sleep every night. I didn't want to live anymore. I started thinking, what did I do to make him do this? I thought, *Is this my fault? Am I unattractive? Am I not satisfying? What did I do wrong?* I was heartbroken.

"I Apologize" by Engelbert—this song broke my heart. I would listen to it at night, and as the days passed, I hopelessly cried and couldn't talk to anyone. Should I apologize? "If I made you cry when I said good-bye, I'm sorry. From the bottom of my heart, dear, I apologize." Should I call him and apologize? "If I caused you pain, I know I'm to blame." Please let me make amends.

No. No. I can't do that. What did I do wrong? Wasn't it him? It's my fault. My love…I lost my love. Please forgive me. No. It's not my fault. I can't apologize. I hate you. I hate you with all my heart. After all, we were more than friends. My pain was unbearable. *I hate you for what you did to our family. But I love you.* My tears fell and felt like they would never stop. My love…I lost the love of my life.

Oh, my love, my darling. I'm sorry, but I want you in Uncle Tony's hands. It's just the thought of you, the very thought of you, my love, in Uncle Tony's hands. And then the phone rang. I picked it up. Silence. "Hello." Silence.

Ritorna me. Cara mia, te amo.

My heart weeps in silence for my lost love. But my love returning to me will not happen.

I eventually proceeded with a divorce. How could I ever be in the same room again with the love of my life and not murder him?

After the divorce and all the heartbreaking tragedy that goes along with watching the love of your life evaporate into thin air, the crying and weeping for the chance to have him back, go to watch the sun set together again, I knew it was my fault, but I decided I was moving my son to Sarasota, Florida, specifically Siesta Beach. I had a nephew down there, and after all, my name is Sara. I wanted to get away from my husband, but more importantly, I wanted to get my son away from all this. I did not want him growing up in this atmosphere and take a chance of him getting involved with something or someone and going to prison. As much as it broke my heart to leave everyone, I decided it was best to let the wind carry my pain away.

Florida Dream

"Oh, Mom, I don't want to go someplace where everybody is sleeping," said my son, referring to Siesta. So I pampered him in a sneaky way and said, "Well, how about if we go down there for a vacation and visit your cousin Pat?" That was okay with him, so come Easter vacation and Spring Break, we went to Siesta Beach. Now, I don't know if you heard anything about Siesta, but it was voted the nicest beach in the whole USA.

I rented a really comfy place on the beach for us to stay, you know, kind of sneakily luring Joey into the move. We spent the days on the beach where they had volleyball, parasailing, and we were also on the Gulf of Mexico. The water was beautiful, and it was eighty-eight degrees, warm and clean. After the beach, we'd shower and change and go into Siesta Village to walk around. Then we'd find a table outside where there was music and have dinner outside every night listening to the music.

When our week was up, he said, "Mom, I don't want to go home. I love it here."

I said, "Pack your bags. We'll go home, sell the house, and move down here."

Now to tell the family, I wanted to ask my son to tell everyone because I knew they would not get angry at him. The family was not happy about it, but they totally understood. Now it was time to go down the Jersey Shore and tell "you know who." *I'll wait until Friday night*, I thought. Our dinners were still on, but my husband wouldn't dare show his face, or he would be decapitated. *I guess I won't call him my husband anymore*, I thought.

I went a little early down to the Paddock because I knew Louie the Killer and Mutsi would be there checking out the restaurant and especially our private room, you know, for safety, and they were surprised to see me so early.

"Louie, I have to talk to you. I need help."

"What's up, babe?"

"Joey and I are moving to Florida." As Louie froze, I explained the situation. He finally understood but didn't think anyone else would. I was determined...maybe *stubborn* is a better word.

"Louie, I need an escape plan. I can't risk running into him and seeing him out with another woman."

"We can take care of it, babe. Let us handle it."

"If I do let you handle it, what would you do?" I asked.

"I take the fifth."

I certainly understood what that meant. "If you do that, you're going to need a fifth," I said, referring to the bottle of Scotch they kept in the cabinet at the office.

As we talked and Louie got me to relax somewhat, "the big guy" got there. I figure I better be extremely nice.

"What?" Screeched Uncle Tony as everyone turned around to look at us and froze. *Should I perhaps cry? I* thought. *Let's have a drink...but Uncle Tony doesn't drink. Well then, I'll have his drink, maybe two more.*

After hours and hours of talking, he finally agreed but only with the understanding that I would check in with the unorganized crew on the west coast of Florida, you know, our gang, and let everybody know where I was, how I was, and where Joey was going to school. "I know you'll need money down there, and I'll come down with you and get you set up."

"Unk, I still have the Bobby G cash, and I'll be okay. I'll call and let everybody know where we are, I promise."

I wasn't going to depend on my ex-husband. I wanted to get out of the cold. I still had the fifty thousand dollars and was okay for a while. I knew if I needed anything, all I had to do was yell and he'd hear me from state to state. They had a way of doing that, you know.

Sarasota, Florida

So that's what we did—sold the house and moved to Siesta Beach, which is in Sarasota, and enrolled him in school. Of course, I had to check out the wrestling programs to pick the area to live in.

And then I found Coach Jones. "You know, there are a lot of kids in his weight category, so I don't know if we have a spot for him. What's his record?" asked the coach.

"He's undefeated in one hundred forty-five pounds on the New Jersey team."

"I want him. Let me know when you come down and the team will help you unpack and set up."

I rented a home in Siesta Beach to give us more time to familiarize ourselves with the area. It was an adorable home in Siesta in the middle of a jungle; it had a nice pool in the backyard, and I enrolled Joey in Sarasota High, where Coach Jones was waiting for him.

Joey became friends with Sean. Sean was a homely little guy with big ears and a big nose, skinny, not much to him. I found out months later by accident that Sean was being bullied at school and that some of the kids were threatening to "get him" after school when Joey stepped in and told them, "If you want to get him, you have to go through me first." Well, being a star wrestler, that didn't happen. They backed down. I was very proud of my son once again.

I was looking to purchase a home, and I had become friends with Margarita, who was a realtor, and she found me a beautiful home in a golf course community, one house off the golf course, which I preferred. I didn't want all those people lurking in my backyard with their sticks. It was at the end of a cul-de-sac, and we were very comfortable and homey there.

With my experience as a court reporter, I was able to get a good job with an Italian guy, Vinny, who was from New York and who owned a court reporting firm. After some more experience with Vinny, I applied for and was accepted as an official court reporter working in the Sarasota County Courthouse, where I worked all the criminal trials, learning more about DNA, friction ridges, and fingerprints, and got to know the Sarasota policemen.

The boys on the wrestling team always came to our house at night because I would cook dinner. And when I cooked, it was like I was cooking for an army. Then one night, they came home and told me a story about a police officer in Siesta Beach who made them lay on the ground handcuffed for an hour while he checked out their identifications. "Did you happen to get his name?" I asked, figuring I'd kill the bastard. My son did read the policeman's name tag and told me what it was. The next day, I went to the police station looking for him. Well, it turns out he was off duty, because he worked all night. But I told the captain what happened the night before, and I threatened if that officer came into court to testify and I was the court reporter, I would make sure I botched up his testimony so badly by continuously interrupting him. I don't know what the captain told that policeman, but to make a long story short, he apologized.

"Mom, can we have a graduation party at the house?" I had this big home with an indoor swimming pool. But we had to make a plan. We would send out invitations for a graduation party that would be held the night before graduation so they all could be with their families for graduation.

It was called preparation. I had a bodyguard at the door. "If you do not have a written invitation, you cannot enter," said the bodyguard. But then all the kids that couldn't enter were sticking around outside. Before you knew it, there were kids galore hanging out in front of the house. And here came the police officer, the same police officer who stopped the boys in Siesta, with a loud speaker. "Anyone not invited to Joe's party, please leave." We were hysterical.

Some of the boys on the wrestling team slept at the house quite often. So that night—these kids were so funny—to the first guy to fall asleep, they painted his fingernails red! When he woke up, he saw his fingernails and went into a panic. I heard him say to somebody, "Do I have the polish anywhere else?" And of course, the response was, "No," but right in the middle of his nose was a big red spot. Well, this poor kid proceeded to go to school and walked up to get his certificate with a big red spot on his nose.

Anyhow, my son's father moved to Sarasota with his new girlfriend—a different girl, not Shitface, whom

I wanted to kill. As Edgar Allan Poe wrote, "I became insane with long intervals of horrible sanity." I was getting the urge to kill him, but I didn't want to hurt my son, so I kept my cool. But I knew I was not going to depend on him for support. Joey saw his dad, but I still couldn't be in the same room as him.

Remembering the nights we listened to Engelbert together and how I fell deeply in love with my husband as Engelbert's music played, I thought of seeking out Engelbert and killing him, hoping that would diminish my hurt. Just a slaughter. I couldn't listen to him any longer, for the memories of Engelbert's music and my husband put extreme hate into my soul. I did not even want child support. I wanted nothing from him. I thought, *I will take care of my son, I will sacrifice everything for my son, and he can see his father whenever he wants to.*

What's the matter with me? Am I stupid? I guess so. If I knew where my so-called girlfriend was whom I saw in my husband's embrace, Shitface, at this point in my life I would have tortured her, and very, very slowly. Better yet, somehow implant her with the Kuru disease, a form of cannibalism where the first sign of impending death is a general debility followed by weakness and the inability to stand and watch her violently shiver with tremors as death eventually ensued.

RAT

The phone rang. "Hello."

Uncle Tony said, "I have a job for you if you're interested."

I didn't want to say too much on the dreadful telephone. "Yes, I'm interested." And he went on to explain, "Billy the Kid and Max will fly into Sarasota tomorrow to tell you all about it. One hundred thousand dollars."

"Holy toledo!"

He proceeded to tell me, "We're in no hurry for this. In fact, we need a little time to set things up. It's a high profile. You need to get acquainted with some software technology that I'll have someone introduce you to. You won't be alone. Billie and Max will drive you where you need to go, stay with you, and when the job is done, they'll come home, but as long as I know we can count on you."

Of course, for one hundred thousand dollars, he could count on me.

Now Billie the Kid was a guy who lived in Peterstown. He was a little guy, and they named him Billie the Kid because he was a second-story man. He would climb in somebody's second-story window and rob them and then climb back down, and they never knew he was there. If a house was one-story, he had this knack—and I don't know how he did it—to get a door unlocked in a matter of seconds.

The little stinker. I remember one time I got locked out of my house and called Billie the Kid to come over and get me in, and he did—real quickly too. He unlocked my front door and had that stupid smile on his face. Billy was Max's mentor. Max was an up-and-coming, and he was in good hands.

So Billy and Max flew in the next day to get me up to speed. It seemed that the job was getting rid of a US Senator from Florida because he defaulted on a million-dollar loan from the mob. I guess the mob was getting organized. About time. Dummies. Maybe he thought because he was a Senator he didn't have to pay back the loan.

But there was a program I had to learn about first. It was RAT or a Remote Access Tool. That was going to be our decoy or trap. In the meantime, the Senator was in Washington DC and was being followed by Uncle Tony's guys everywhere he went. They wanted to know everything about him, his family, and if he had a girl-friend. Everything. I would perform voodoo! No, I'm only kidding.

During the next few months, I avoided my husband, but he didn't live far from us, so Joey saw him often. His older brother and two sisters also moved down to Sarasota. It was a family thing. But as Pope Francis said, "Diplomacy is a work of small steps."

Back Orifice

I was spending my time learning about the RAT, an intrusive computer program. RAT gives an intruder (me) invisible administrative control or physical access over a target computer. It's a malware program installed without someone's knowledge and can be sent through the back door of a computer by an e-mail. So if I sent the Senator an e-mail and he opened it up, he would unknowingly give me access to his computer, and I would be able to manage his files and have image con-trol over his computer or watch what he was doing. I would also be able to record anything that was going on in his office. I literally would be able to do anything with his computer that I chose to do, which means I could also delete an e-mail that I sent him, and with one key word I would be able to instruct his machine to reformat his hard drive, leaving no trace of my attack.

The RAT I was thinking of using was called Back Orifice, which was created by The Cult of the Dead Cow, and all I needed was his personal e-mail address, which the unorganized guys were getting for me.

My plan was to gain access to the Senator's computer beforehand, and then on Halloween, when I would dress up as a clown, which I told Chaz he should have done, I would e-mail him, an e-mail that was supposedly to be from his girlfriend, which the Unwise Guys told me he had and who she was. Then I would immediately reformat his computer, leaving no trace of my e-mail, and do my job so I could proceed to get my one hundred thousand dollars. Sticks and stones may break my bones, but words are gonna hurt you. I'm just sayin' because by this time, I knew from his computer that he was making plans to come back to Florida from Washington DC, for a few days, and I was going to do this in Florida.

Time was getting close, and I thought, *Concentrate. No mistakes will be made.* "But first we have to scout out a place for a body dump, and then we can drive over to the Capitol building in Tallahassee to check out the building, his office, and which exit he would be leaving the building, sort of getting a lay of the land. We want everything covered," I said to the guys.

We drove to Myaaka, but it was getting too developed for a body dump. Someone might see us digging on their property and call the police.

"This is your state," Billy said. "Where do you want to go next?"

"How about the Everglades? We won't have to dig."

We gassed up the van and got onto Florida Route 72 and drove East toward the Florida Everglades, or Liquid Land, as we call it, where the gators and snakes were rampant. There were even Burmese pythons and boas. No digging for us as we drove through the Panther Habitat.

"Max, watch your speed," said Billy. "We don't want to get pulled over by the police."

"No worries. I'm on climate control," replied Max.

"You're not on climate control, buddy," responded Billy. "You're on cruise control."

"This is the area we want," I told Billy as we pulled the van off to the side of the road in a quiet rest area. We got out to walk around and canvass the area, acting like tourists. As we walked, we came across a snake sunbathing. Billy got so scared he screamed.

"Come on, Billy, let's walk through the mud."

"You crazy?" said Billy. "Let's not and say we didn't." Max was laughing so hard I thought he was going to wet his pants.

"Billy, Billy, Billy." I smiled.

Max said, "I got a joke for you. A young boy went with his dad to see a litter of kittens. When they went home, he told his mother that there were two boy kittens and two girl kittens. The mother asked, 'How did you know?' The boy answered, 'Daddy picked them up and looked underneath. I think it's printed on the bottom.'"

We finally found a spot that was hidden from the public, and now all we had to do was remember where we were, as we were in no way going to write anything down to incriminate us.

Max said, "Let's go back to your house, get something to eat, get a good night's rest, and then we can go to the Capitol tomorrow. Give us a fresh start. How's that sound?"

"Sounds good to me," said Billy.

"You guys. Okay." Now back to Sarasota to prepare. This was a masterpiece of a plan.

The next morning, Max was ready. "Okay, everybody, rise and shine. It's killin' time."

After we scouted out the Florida Capitol the next day, Billy and Max went back to Jersey to tell Uncle Tony about our plan, and they would make arrangements to return to Florida when the Senator was leaving DC. So far, everything was under control. I felt like the emissary of Satan.

It's Killin' Time for Real

The day finally arrived when the super spies in Jersey, Mike and Angelo, who had been following the Senator, and whom I grew up with and trusted, said the Senator was coming home to Florida for a break from DC. Joey made arrangements to stay with his dad for a few days, so I didn't have to worry about him. Billy and Max came back to Florida; and Billy, Max, and I drove to Tallahassee with my computer and my clown outfit, but we decided to sleep in Billy's van, so there was no trace of us being there in a hotel or motel.

As I put my head back and closed my eyes, I thought of our song by Engelbert, "From Here to Eternity." The lyrics kept running in my head, "Now I'm alone with only a memory. My empty arms will never know why," as my tears slid silently down my face.

The next morning, with our sunglasses and light-weight shirts with hoods on, we walked back around the Capitol. Billy brought a sketch of the building showing entrances and exits so we knew that in advance, but I wanted to actually see them in person.

"Tomorrow is Halloween," I said. "We'll do it and get out of here." As we went back out to the van, I connected the computer, checked once again my access to the Senator's computer with the RAT, making sure I could see and hear everything that was happening in his office. It was working just fine. This was a secret to keep secret, for sure.

The next morning, I changed into a clown in the ladies' room of a gas station and thought about how I couldn't wait to get home to shower. As I got into the car, Max looked at me in my clown costume and started laughing. "I was born to be brutal," I said.

We're So Smart

I also installed a program on my iPhone that's a mobile tracking device. It was originally programmed to track a cheating spouse where you could actually hear and record their conversations and track their text messages. The users of this program, which I won't give the name, say they use it to prove that their spouse or lover is not cheating on them. Whatever. I also found it on the Internet. Check it out yourself. I was able to keep track of the Senator's girlfriend while we were very busy with her boyfriend.

When we got to the Capitol building, we drove to the back of the building where we knew the Senator would be exiting. I opened up my computer, and with the RAT, I sent the Senator a message from his girlfriend, asking him to meet her at their meeting spot, which Angelo and Mike found out by following him previously. They discovered it was one of those long-term hotel rentals. By our iPhone mobile tracking device, we knew she would be at the hairdresser's and would not get in our way. This was our day of "bamboozle" as Billy put it.

The Senator's response was immediate. He would leave the Senate Office Building in ten minutes and would be right over. This is what we, the American people, are paying for—an idiot that we voted into power.

Of course, the girlfriend didn't get the message because we had programmed RAT to send us the response, and once that happened, we immediately deleted all traces of us from his computer and reformatted the Senator's hard drive so there would be no tracking it back to us.

When the Senator left the building, we were behind him. Of course, he did not have any security with him because he didn't want anyone to know where he was going. When he arrived at the long-term hotel that he kept an apartment in, he pulled around the back, as did we, and we watched as he parked his car, got out, and went in through the back door.

Billy and his protégé, Max, stayed in the car. I waited, holding my breath, and then went in the back door too. His room was close to the back door. I was getting nervous. Would I be able to achieve my goal? Huh! What do you think? I thought about my husband and Shitface again, and I was ready. I wanted to kill.

The hallway was quiet. There wasn't a soul in sight. As I walked up to his door and knocked. "Pizza," I said. The plan was to bring an empty pizza box with my 9mm Glock with silencer attached hidden in the box.

Uncle Tony and the Maniacs wanted the Senator dead because, as was explained to me in a little more detail, "he double-crossed us on a payout." Apparently, aside from borrowing all that money, they backed the Senator when he was running for office and helped him get elected, and then he misled them, borrowed more money, did not back their gambling and prostitution establishments, which ultimately were closed. Guys were arrested and subsequently imprisoned, and in their words, the Senator committed treason.

As the door to the room opened, the Senator looked at the clown costume and started laughing. "I didn't order pizza." With that, I quickly pushed the door open, stepped into the room, opened the box, took out my Glock, and silently shot him between the eyes. "All is forgiven," I said.

He looked at me, and I was the last thing he saw. I could see all signs of life leaving him, as I thought, *Too bad, Senator. You could have shared the profits and not kept the millions of dollars for yourself, and there would be nothing to forgive.*

Now I had to get him out of here. No telephones. Our gang was adamant about that, so I exited, turned right, and the door out of the building was right there. And so were Billy and Max. I opened the door, and I could see them waiting for me. As I motioned for them to come inside, I checked the hallway again. Someone was coming.

"Wait," I said as I closed the door so they wouldn't be spotted.

"Hello. Nice costume."

He should know, I thought as he turned the corner.

"Okay, guys, hurry."

Billy and Max came in, and we went back in the room to maneuver the body out. *My God, he was bloody. Ugh!* I thought.

I cleaned him up a bit. "Put this on him," I said. I brought a facial mask with me and put it on the Senator so just in case someone saw us they would think the guy was drunk, not dead. They wouldn't be able to recognize him, they couldn't recognize me as the clown, and Billy and Max would simply turn away. We held him up, one on either side, and walked him out to the car while Max opened the back door and placed him back there.

That accomplished, I went back into the room to clean up any mess I might have made—blood spatter, DNA, fingerprints. I made sure everything was so clean that they wouldn't be able to find any trace of blood, even with luminol testing.

Back out to the car, we pulled away slowly so as to not attract attention. By this time, it was dusk, and we welcomed sunset. We needed to get back out to the Everglades and do a body dump—in other words, feed the gators and get the hell out of there.

When we found our spot, we maneuvered the car around for further concealment of the dead body. We were able to get the body out of the car with no problem. I took his mask off, dumped him, and watched him sink. Hopefully the gators would eat him quickly, and if he was ever discovered, his remains, if any, would be severely degraded and unidentifiable.

On our drive back, Max said, "A man and a woman met aboard a cruise ship."

"Max, shut up." Billy tried to interrupt him.

Max continued, "'I feel it's only fair to warn you that I'm a real golf nut,' the man told the woman. 'I live, eat, and sleep the game.'"

"Oh, damn," said Billy. "He's never going to shut up."

"'Well,' the woman said, 'since you're being honest, so will I. I'm a hooker.' The man said, 'I see. Well, it's probably because you're not keeping your wrists straight when you hit the ball,'" Max said.

The next day, November 1, Billy and Max went back to Jersey, and I was reading in the newspaper about a United States Senator in Florida who did not return home last night and was missing. They called in the FBI to investigate. *Maybe they'll investigate his girlfriend,* I thought.

Now I just had to collect my one hundred thousand dollars and buy my son a new car.

7

In Silence I Grieve

As time went on, I thought about the men I killed and the one that got away…my husband, the love of my life.

I wondered if I was offered another brutal job if I would take it. Of course, I would. I was getting used to this kind of life and so far was able to clean up my mess and not get caught.

When I got back to town, the kids called me, Joey, and his brothers and sisters. Their dad had gotten sick and was diagnosed with cancer. I was sorry to hear it. If he would have come home that night and I killed him, it would have been quicker for him instead of the chemotherapy treatment plan the doctor recommended.

When he was undergoing chemo, he lost his appetite, so I cooked the food I knew he liked and brought it to him, trying to build him up. If I could only build him up to be strong again, I'd punch him in the nose. But nothing seemed to be working. He was getting weaker and weaker, losing more and more weight. In time, he did pass away, and it was so sad—sad to see what the kids were going through and sad to know this chapter of my life had come to an end.

A part of me died with him as I thought of the quote by Lord Byron "In silence I grieve. That my heart could forget. Thy spirit deceive. If I should meet Thee after long years, how should I greet thee? With silence and tears."

My friend Frank, who I grew up with, lived in Sarasota, and we would get together to go out for pizza. We found this wonderful pizza place where the pizza crust was absolutely perfect, you know, good old Jersey pizza. This was our Saturday night pizza place. And we heard of another spot right off Tamiami Trail or US 41 and Tenth Street called the Broadway Bar, and inside was The Starlite Room. On Monday nights, they had entertainment, a singer by the name of John.

So one Monday night, we decided to go and check him out because we heard he sang Sinatra, Dean

Martin, and Cole Porter tunes, and we liked that kind of soft music that relaxed you. As we sat there and the music started, I was amazed. "Frank, I think I'm hearing things. Is Sinatra still alive? Where is this beautiful music coming from?"

"It looks like John is singing. Maybe he's just moving his lips in time with the song." As we continued to stare, we discovered that John was really singing.

"Want to dance?" I asked Frank.

As it turned out, John and I had the same last name, and so we had to figure out if we were related. I'm keeping it a secret and not telling you the results.

Anyway, getting back to Louie the Killer, he was coming to Sarasota and staying at the house one weekend of the month to check on me, and we started cooking and baking all day, which kept us very busy. I was taking more baking classes and cake decorating and would make up batches of delicious icings. It was just anything to keep ourselves busy—French icing, buttercream, chocolate, different cakes and cookies.

One day a few years later, I was in a good mood because I got Louie good with buttercream icing, and the telephone rang. A while back, I had gotten a call from a friend of one of my cousins in Arizona, Steve, whom I knew for many years, and he said he was coming to Florida on business.

Scumbag

"Hi, Sara, I'm in Fort Lauderdale on business, and if you're free for the weekend, I can drive to Sarasota to see you."

"Well, I have company in from Jersey, but I'm sure he wouldn't mind, and I know he'd like to meet you." I figured if I didn't like him, Louie would throw him away with the trash, so I gave Steve driving directions from Fort Lauderdale to Sarasota, actually driving the Senator's murder route in the Everglades.

The next morning, Louie sat at the table and waited. When Steve finally got there, Louie sat there. And Louie sat there some more. We talked...and Louie sat there some more.

"Let's go eat." There was a fabulous restaurant at the marina with great atmosphere. *Here we come! All three of us.*

Afterward, Steve went to a hotel and went back to Phoenix the following day.

Over the next year, Steve and I developed a close relationship. He would fly into town a couple of weekends a month. Joey was grown. He graduated from Sarasota High School, and was getting ready to go to college... Gatorland, as I call it. University of Florida. Memories of the prince, Bobby Genovese, and the Senator were behind me, and I was looking toward the future. I bought Joey a motorcycle because he had been riding since high school, and I figured parking was easier for him at college with a motorcycle.

We even started going to the Gators home football games. "Mom, the Gators are playing at home on Saturday. Do you want to come to the game?"

"Sure. I'll get tickets." I went online where I had previously found all my murder equipment and bought season tickets for all the Gator home football games. Early Saturday morning I drove to the university, and when I got there to pick him up, Joey said, "Let's take my bike. Easier parking."

"No way. I'm not getting on a bike with you."

Well, we drove and drove and could not find parking, so I finally said, "Okay, let's go get your bike." He was in his glory. As I sat on the back and we put our helmets on, I said, "Remember, this is your mother back here."

Then one weekend, Steve called from the airport. "I'm in town."

S——t, I thought but didn't say it out loud.

"I'll take a cab."

What the hell? I wasn't going to pick him up, but when he got to the house, I was happy to see him. We went out to dinner and ordered a bottle of wine, and then Steve took my hand and said, "Sara, would you marry me?"

Oh, boy, I thought to myself. Why? Why would I want to do this? I mean, I like revenge, but this might be too much. I was nice to him, beat around the bush somewhat, and he asked me to think about it. He stayed for the weekend, and when he went back to Arizona, I talked to my son and told him about Steve's proposal. We talked, and he said he didn't want me being alone, and the only thing he said that sank in the whole night we talked was, "I always wanted to see the West Coast, and with your job as a court reporter, you can work anywhere." Of course, he made sense, and the next day, I called Steve back and accepted his marriage proposal.

Arizona

Moving west to Arizona was an interesting endeavor. I kept my home in Sarasota thinking I would use it for vacations and visiting all my friends.

For a while, there was a big investigation on the missing Florida Senator, but there were no clues. Hahahaha. Me and my one hundred thousand dollars were very happy together.

My son and I moved into Steve's house in Scottsdale and got ready for the wedding. It was fun, I guess, nothing fantastic. Guess I was just not into weddings anymore. And Joey also enrolled in college out there.

I had never been out West, and Scottsdale was an interesting place. *I wonder if the "gangstas" would need any work done out here?* But I was only thinking to myself because Joey had no idea about any of this. I needed to get the lay of the land, so to speak.

Steve's house was beautiful. It had tile floors, a rec room with a built-in bar, a beautiful fireplace, and a large dining room. The backyard had a built-in pool and a grill, and it overlooked the serene desert, which had coyotes. I had never seen a coyote before. One night, Joey left his shoes outside, and when we woke up, one of his shoes was missing, so we walked behind the house in the desert and found it shredded to pieces. "Guess I won't wear these anymore," he said.

We had an outdoor wedding at the house with a four-piece mariachi band. Joey was the best man. It was fun.

Getting acquainted with Scottsdale was also fun. Old Town Scottsdale was so quaint with places like the Pink Pony. You could still tie your horse outside and water him. Then there was Rawhide. What I loved most was that you could carry a gun out in the open. That's right. It was allowed as long as it wasn't concealed because for that you needed a concealed weapons permit. Scottsdale was for me. Yes, I did eventually get my concealed weapons permit and I did carry a gun.

The first Saturday in May is Kentucky Derby time. A group of us would get together and go to Kentucky for the Derby weekend. That was fun. Even wearing those big funny-looking hats was fun.

I started working as a fill-in court reporter at the Maricopa County Courthouse covering different courts with different judges. I got to be friends with one of the judges, who was Italian but came from New York. According to his secretary, Jane, he was forbidden to drink coffee before going into the courtroom in the mornings because it "sped him up," and believe me, I didn't want him in that condition.

One morning, we went into court. The clerk said, "All rise," and then the judge took his seat at the bench and started talking. "Blah-blah-blah-blah." Everything was so fast that I didn't understand a word he said.

"Excuse me, Your Honor, I think there's something wrong with my machine. Can we take a break?" With that, as we walked back to his office, he said to me, "I snuck coffee this morning, but don't tell Jane."

"You what? No wonder why I couldn't understand you. I'm telling." He was on a coffee high.

We walked in the office. Jane looked up, and I said, "He drank coffee this morning."

The fit hit the shan. After Jane got finished with him, I said, "Go to your room. Ten-minute timeout." He walked to his office, and I closed the door behind him until he had time to come off his coffee high.

A few months later, one of the magistrates I worked with often was made a judge and asked me if I would accept a permanent position as his court reporter, which I did. Some of Uncle Tony's friends lived in Scottsdale, and we got together with them every so often. They weren't crazy about Steve, so I didn't punish them too much by bringing Steve with me, and by this time, Chaz was being released from prison. I had gone to see him often in prison, and we wrote to each other. He was able to call from time to time, and we remained friends throughout the years.

As a court reporter, you have to keep up your continuing education credits of thirty hours every three years, or you lose your certification with our national organization. If you're an official, you need your certification, so I tried to pick something interesting to attend instead of the usual boring meetings and found out I could go out with the SWAT team in Phoenix. I spoke with one of the SWAT team officers who testified in our courtroom, and he arranged for me to go out with them that Friday night.

"Sara," my judge said. "You're crazy. You could get hurt." He should know.

It just so happened they wound up taking down a gang that night. How exciting was this? We were called out to a gang shooting—actually two gangs shooting at each other.

"Sara, stay in the truck."

"My goodness. Was this exciting!"

But that was the second time I had come in contact with gangs. One morning, I parked my car to go into work, and when I opened my door, there was a gang fight right by my car door. I said, "Excuse me, boys," as I moved them aside and proceeded to go to work.

But aside from the SWAT team, there was also the medical helicopter. Very interesting. We flew up and down the Interstate to see if there were any accidents and if anyone needed help.

And then I came across autopsies. Disgusting. The Chief Medical Examiner, Dr. Kane, was in court one day testifying about an autopsy performed on a murder victim.

"An autopsy was performed on January twenty-ninth. There were ten separate knife wounds—one in the forehead, three in the left front neck. When I say left and right, that's to the body, my left, my right. If it's left front neck, it's the victim's left front neck. Left chest above the nipple, left inner forearm just below the elbow, left outside forearm between the elbow and the wrist, left upper biceps. These stab wounds caused incised wounds of the heart, right and left lungs, esophagus, the left jugular vein, and the left subclavian artery. There were also rib fractures, secondary to the stab wounds with regard to the amount of force used."

Doc, I wanted to say, *slow the hell down*. I never heard some of these words before.

"There was also postmortem, that is after death, trauma to the right and left leg and the right and left shoulder. The body was identified as the victim's by a positive match on the dental records."

The prosecutor asked, "So when you first did your physical examination of the body, what did you see when the body was taken out of the bag?"

The Chief Medical Examiner responded, "What I saw was a decomposing Caucasian male. The post-mortem stiffening of the body was absent. Lividity or settling of the blood was present but fixed, meaning it wasn't changeable. There were early decomposition changes present, including maggot infestation."

Ugh! What a disgusting job he has.

"The face was red-green and discolored with subcu-taneous gas formation and skin slippage, or the skin was actually falling off the surface. There was drying artifact seen on the hands and feet and face. There was drying of the hands and feet, early mummification we call it. And there was also maggots involving the face and in the stab wounds."

"Was there also maggot infestation, for example, in the extremities, such as the ears?"

"Yes. There were maggot holes. We actually call them chew areas on the ears."

"And are maggots fly larvae that eat flesh?"

"Yes," said Dr. Kane.

Hell, I thought, *this is good to know. Maggots that eat flesh? Maybe I can start collecting them. Never can tell when I'll need them.*

"What did you measure to be the, I guess, the length of the body and the weight?"

"The length of the body was seventy-one inches long, and the weight was a hundred and twenty-four pounds."

"So now at this point, what was the pathologic diagnosis?"

"The first diagnosis was that of multiple stab wounds. There were incisions or stab wounds of the heart, the right and left lungs, the esophagus, left jugular vein, and the left subclavian artery, and there were also rib fractures."

And Dr. Kane went on to describe rib fractures and the force required to fracture a bone.

The prosecutor apparently wanted the jury to suffer with this testimony. He continued, "Could you now explain the various wounds into George Daniels' anatomy?"

I mean, I'm not dainty, but this was disgusting, even for a killer.

The testimony continued, "There was a stab wound to the top of the head near the hairline. It was superficial but didn't enter the skull. There were also three stab wounds to the side of the neck. One entered the deeper structures and actually incised the left jugular vein on the side of the neck and also the left subclavian artery. It's a major vein, and if it's opened up, a lot of blood would come out as long as the heart's pumping."

"And what was the directionality of the stab?"

"The directionality is in relationship to the decedent's left and right and top and bottom. When I say downward, it's from his top toward his feet. The path of this wound was downward, slightly left to right and slightly front to back."

As the Chief Medical Examiner testified, he spoke to the jurors as he was asked to explain decomposition of a body and the odor a body will produce.

"What produces these odors? Let's go the other extreme and say it's a hot day and the sun is on the body and you know the body is getting sun, let's say it's summer, what produces the odors?"

"The body forms methane gas, like the smell of rotten eggs and that sort of thing, the putrid fraction on the inside and the bowel, and that makes the body swell and bloat. Whereas when you cool it, the bacteria slow down and are unable to produce the gas."

The Chief Medical Examiner finished his testimony and was excused to go back to his rotten, odor-inflicted office and dead bodies.

Next, the prosecutor called the crime scene investigator. *My, my,* I thought, *I'm sure learning a lot.*

The prosecutor asked, "Did you do luminol testing?"

"Yes, I did. That was the second chemical test that I did. The first chemical test I did was called a phenolphthalein test."

"And as a result of the phenolphthalein test, did you find positive results?"

"Yes, in each and every one of these blood sites. The second type of test is called luminol. It's a chemical test, also a presumptive for latent blood, that is, blood that has either been washed away, wiped away, or is not readily visible because of the surfaces.

"Luminol is used in a global application. That is, it's sprayed on all surfaces, floors, ceilings, walls, and all furnishings. In the presence of blood, it will produce a luminescence. The color is blue-white in appearance, and this light is very weak, but it is capable of being photographed. What we are looking at here is a photo of the living room floor. You see the stool in the middle of the living room floor? The reaction area is blue-white. And in the upper center of the photograph is the open kitchen door. The blue-white reactions are a white pattern that extends from the door to the bottom of the photograph. A white pattern would be any pattern that results from mechanical distribution of the stain."

"Wiping it?"

"Exactly."

"Is there anything about this white pattern to you as a crime scene analyst that is indicative of some particular mechanism, mop, towel, whatever?"

"It could be interpreted as a mop wipe."

So, I thought to myself, *the defendant tried to mop up the blood after killing his boyfriend, and luminol testing of the house uncovered the crime scene. Hmm, guess he didn't use the right chemical to clean. I'll have to remember this.*

Well, ladies and gentlemen, I got through this awful procedure. When we took a break and I went back into my office, guess who was sitting there waiting for me? You got it—Dr. Kane. "If this is ever ordered, you're going to transcribe it," I told him. He laughed. Did he think I was not serious?

"Have you ever been to an autopsy?"

"What? An autopsy? Why would I go to an autopsy, especially after hearing your testimony? Was this actually your goal in life to do this, to be a medical examiner and work on dead bodies?" said intelligent me.

"You can get your continuing education credits," said Dr. Kane.

"Count me in."

Now this turned out to be awesome. When I went that Saturday morning, he gave me a gown and something to put over my head and feet, like a doctor's outfit in the operating room. I felt like an alien. Okay, now what?

"If you can last ten minutes with the smell," said Dr. Kane, "you'll be okay." As he stood over the body and pressed the recorder to start recording, he explained what he was doing, his eyes focused on mine.

I was intrigued as he made the first cut. I thought it had to be at least ten minutes by now, but when I looked at the clock, it was thirty seconds. He cut the V in the dead man's chest with a saw, opened him up, took out his heart, his liver, his kidneys, and weighed each before placing them in separate identifiable bags. I smelled the horrible aroma of the room as I looked at the clock.

What's this? He had a penis pump! Oh, my God! This is the most disgusting thing I ever saw, I thought as I watched him remove it. My ten minutes was up.

Now it was time for the brain. My pal, the Chief Medical Examiner, sawed the top of the forehead down to the ears as he pulled the flesh down to expose the brain. *Well, there it is. The brain is sitting there in the head. In broad daylight. Where else would it be, Sara?* I thought. *Oh my, now he's taking the brain out. With his hands.* He brought it over to another table to examine it and sliced off a piece of brain to test.

When he finished examining, weighing, taking samples of everything, he put all the parts back inside the corpse and stitched him up.

"Ready for another one?" he asked.

"Move aside and let the lady go through," I said.

After three autopsies in total, we each went to separate quarters, showered and changed into clean, non-smelling clothes, and met in the lobby.

"Want to have lunch and go to a ball game?" Well, my husband was working out of town this weekend, and I had nothing else to do, so off we went. *How do you eat after three autopsies*, I thought. *Guess I'll find out.*

8

Friends

During all this time, I was in constant touch with all my friends in New Jersey that I knew from kindergarten, and some even before that, like Frank, Angelo, Louise, Chaz, Mike, Clams, my very close girl-friends Cindy, Carol, Annie, and the rest of the girls. And through my sisters and brothers-in-law, I also kept up-to-date on the people from the neighborhood that were more their age and, of course, my dad's friend Jimmy who lived by me in Scottsdale.

Chaz was out of prison and called, saying, he was coming to Arizona to visit me and the Unwise Guy Jimmy. He wanted to meet Steve, and so I invited him to stay at the house. After all, we were friends since we could walk, and he wanted to meet Shithead—or Scumbag, as the case may be. Steve, or Scumbag, was a little frightened of Chaz because all he had to do was look at you and you would go into an immediate Stroke—that word is capitalized.

The first night Chaz came in, my dad's friend Jimmy who lived down the street from me in Scottsdale came over, and we all went to Old Town Scottsdale to have dinner. Then we took a ride out to Rawhide...remember that old song? Well, they had a little cowboy town called Rawhide, and everybody's packin'.

After we got back to the house, Chaz and Scumbag were sitting at the bar in the rec room. I was doing something in the kitchen, and I heard Chaz say to Scumbag, "If you ever do anything to hurt her, I'll kill you."

I ran out of the kitchen, into the rec room, and I saw Steve sort of paralyzed. It was heart attack in action—his face turned white, but he survived. The next night, Chaz went back home to New Jersey, and Stevie boy was happy.

I became friends with an Indian chief on the Indian Reservation named Bill, who would come into our courtroom a lot, and through him I met TC, a cowboy who owned a buffalo ranch by me. When my husband was out of town, I would go hang out there and ride his horses. TC owned Harvey Wallbanger, his pet buffalo, and one day TC disappeared. Nobody could find him.

"Search is on. Look through all the barns, look in the stalls for the food, and look by all the horses," said Bill, "just in case he's lying somewhere." TC was eventually found out on the range sleeping on top of Harvey. Harvey was trained but would only listen to TC, so we had no choice but to leave the two of them alone. They used to do tricks together where TC would lie on the ground and Harvey would lie on top of him but not touch him. Amazing.

"I'm not going by TC with Harvey around." Harvey was like a guard dog. Stay away from my daddy and let him sleep!

After a few years in Scottsdale, I found out that Steve, to my surprise, was an alcoholic. About a few years had passed, and he came home so drunk one night and came after me. He broke my feet by holding my arms and jumping on my feet—he was a big man after all. With broken feet, there was not much I could do, so I called the police and had him arrested. They came out to the house and saw the condition my feet were in, took a report, and booked him.

When I went into work the next day, my judge saw my feet, and I told him what happened, he said, "Sara, you have to get a restraining order so this doesn't happen again. You've seen this time after time in our courtroom where the wife feels sorry for her husband, doesn't get a restraining order, and he does it again."

"I guess you're right, Judge." He was right. I did watch this happen time after time and couldn't understand why a woman would go back to live with her husband and not file charges against him.

"Go home. You shouldn't be in work now. I'll help you call the right people to get him out of the house."

So I proceeded, with my judge's help, to go through the process of getting him the hell out of my life—legally, at this point.

"Jimmy," my dad's friend that lived by me, I said. "I need you."

The next day, I started looking through some papers Scumbag had in his desk, medical records from his doctor. When I came across one in particular, I said, "S——t. How did I not realize this?"

I called a girlfriend, Margie, whom I worked with at the courthouse. "Margie, can you come to the house after work? I found something, a questionnaire from the doctor's office, and I need another opinion." I figured that was all I'd tell her and see what she thought.

When she arrived, I gave her the medical questionnaire. "It says here, 'Are you sexually active?' And the response is yes. Next question"—Margie was reading— "'If the answer is yes, is your partner a male or female?' Answer—male."

"Sara, if this is a guy, he's definitely gay. Who is it?"

"How could this happen? This is my husband. This is Scumbag," I said as I sat there bandaged and bruised.

Chaz

Joey was back East by now, and he went to Washington DC and met his brothers and sisters out there, so I was totally alone and didn't know what to do. I called Jimmy again, and he came over and kept me company that night. Miraculously, the next morning, the phone rang.

"*Princesa*, what happened?" Chaz said.

"How did you find out? And how did you find out so quickly?"

"I'm coming back. I'll be landing at noon tomorrow. Jimmy will pick me up, and I'll be there."

I was afraid for Chaz, afraid he would do something to get in trouble again, and I told him, "I'm fine. Stay home." But there was nothing I could say to change his mind, so my killer friend, whom everybody was deathly afraid of came to my rescue, came to Arizona from New Jersey the next day to stay with me, comfort me, and protect me. He stayed for three weeks cleaning the house, cooking, shopping. He did everything, and I'm indebted to him for the rest of my life. That's what you call a friend.

Of course, I went through a divorce, which my judge helped me get through. After Chaz left, I knew I would be moving soon to the Washington DC area where the kids were and spoke with my judge about it. "I understand, Sara. You have to do what's best for you."

We divorced, and I saved Chaz's life. After some time, I knew, for I was able to read Chaz's mind—what do they call it? Telepathy?

So one night, before moving back east; it was ten thirty at night. The streets of Scottsdale were quiet, and I went back to the house, and I killed the bastard. This was the kill that brought me happiness. "All is forgiven," I told him. I just wish I had tortured him first, but I just couldn't risk it.

After my divorce, Dr. Kane and I became good friends. When my feet were broken, I confided in him about what happened because after five weeks, I wanted him to cut the casts off my feet. He said he couldn't do that but made it a lot more comfortable for me by cutting holes in the casts where it was brushing up against my ankles. So being the Chief Medical Examiner, I knew Dr. Kane would be doing the autopsy on the body of Scumbag, and I knew he would cover up my mess if it became a problem.

I left Arizona and did not go back for the funeral. I did not call to say I was sorry. I wasn't sorry. If I didn't do what I did, Chaz would have done it, and three strikes and you would be out. Chaz would have spent the rest of his life in prison.

Joey said, "Mom, we're coming to pick you up. We're all coming, and we'll make a vacation out of it and get you home."

Joey's sister said, "Yes, we can go see the Grand Canyon."

Joey said, "And we'll drive to New Mexico to go whitewater rafting on the Taos River. I always wanted to do that."

What fun! I thought. "Sounds good to me," I said.

And what a wonderful, fun trip it was getting back to the East Coast and back to my neck of the woods and staying with Joey and his brother, who were living a few blocks from their two sisters and a brother. One girl was still in Florida. I wanted to work, and this was a good place for me. I'd look for a job.

As I read our Journal of Court Reporting for jobs in the Washington DC area, I went back to depositions and civil work until something came along in one of the courts or up on Capitol Hill. I worked with a woman named Carol for a while, and she was a trip. Then I saw in the Court Reporting Journal an opening in the US District Court in Washington DC. *Oh my, this is for me. What's the telephone number?*

"Hello, my name is Sara Bocelli, and I'm a court reporter." I almost said, "I'm a killer for hire."

"I'd like to apply for the job."

"Oh, it's with the chief judge? Wonderful."

US District Court, Washington DC

I went through my experience in court reporting, not killing, and they scheduled me to go in the following day to take what was known as a real-time test. You connect your court reporting machine to your computer by real-time cables. As the court reporter is writing on their machine, what you write (remember this is by sound, it's not English) goes from your machine into your computer, through your dictionary, and gets displayed on your computer screen in English. When you're writing real-time in the courtroom with a judge, your computer is connected by cables to the judge's computer on his desk. This enables the judge to read the proceedings.

If an attorney makes an objection about the question being asked of a witness, the judge can go back, read the question, and make an intelligent decision. In other words, they need us.

So they wanted to see how capable I was of taking down testimony. This was a definite maybe. When I got there at ten o'clock the next morning with all my equipment, it seemed there were four other people there already to take the same test, and they were waiting for one more. I told the supervisor, "Just tell her the job is taken."

"Set up and get ready because you have three five-minute tests on your machine, and then you have a written exam." I was there until four o'clock in the afternoon.

Three tests later and an interview with the chief judge, I drove home exhausted thinking I'd rather be a killer than go through this again. But the next day, the supervisor called and offered me the position of official court reporter in the US District Court, Washington DC, where I immediately drove back, met with her, and was sworn in.

What a place! I thought. *This is where I could get the knowledge to make my real job as a killer, the job that I totally enjoy, the job that I make top salary easier.*

"Uncle Tony, guess where I am!"

I worked a day on Capitol Hill in an open session on Afghanistan, I worked a day at the National Archives with the chief judge for their opening ceremony when construction was completed, and I did a memorial at the Pentagon for 9/11. This one was truly heartbreaking. I was in tears. The ceremony was outside on the grounds of the Pentagon. The main speaker got up and said:

"We are here in the United States, a nation which is the leader of the Free World. We are here to begin our two-day celebration by remembering and by honoring the people who lost their lives in nine-eleven, a hundred yards from here, defending their freedom. I am going to welcome our special guests and proceed with the program and ask for everybody's cooperation. As a civilian aide to the Secretary of the Army, it is a distinct honor to represent the Secretary and our United States Army on this occasion, on this solemn occasion where six months ago heinous acts were directed against not only the United States but also those who stand for similar values around the world.

"At this moment when exactly six months ago terrorists hit the Pentagon complex with a plane filled with innocent people, which exploded, we're going to stand in a moment of silence, but we will answer that silence with our prayer for peace.

"So at this point, I would ask that we reflect and remember those who give their lives for this country to defend it. We don't respond to terrorism with fear. We respond with optimism, we respond with faith, and we respond with a pursuit of a better future. May this ceremony forever remind us in the years to come of those who paid the ultimate sacrifice over the skies of Pennsylvania at the World Trade Center and here at the Pentagon.

'This is the greatest country on the face of the earth. It is the country that stands for freedom, that fights for freedom, that gives its sons and daughters freedom, and your support and your presence and your willingness to come this far on this kind of a day is a marvelous thing.

"The dignity of the human being must be the essence of our religious conviction in the United States, a country whose governance was based on faith. That faith was the essence of democracy. I have found political ignorance to be a significant threat to the stability to our safety, to our welfare. All of us are today deeply concerned about the bloodshed and violence that now characterize the Middle East. I respectfully suggest that political ignorance has played a significant role in contributing to that tragedy. Let me illustrate that point with only one vivid example.

"Our responsibility as well as to champion democracy is the political expression of our faith. Our task is a challenge, but let us not be misled by the headlines. Freedom is contagious. A higher proportion and a greater number of the world population are today living in Democracies or near Democracies than ever before in the history of the world. Only China with its immense population, and here there are some signs to the contrary as well, and a few of the Islamic countries are in prison today by the failures of ignorance.

"Let us then pray and work to turn the twenty-first century into the century for democracy and human dignity, and that to me is the essence of the call for education."

With that, everyone bowed their head, and we had a moment of silence.

The rest of the time, I worked at our courthouse. I actually had a big office where I set up my desk, a table and chairs, a small refrigerator, and a coffee machine. One early Monday morning, I had come back to DC after a seminar in San Diego—and driving down to Tijuana, Mexico, to bring back some Cuban cigars—and I was on the back elevator that judges and court employees use and saw our Chief Judge. "Hi, Judge. I have something for you," as I handed him a cigar.

"Sara, this is a Cuban cigar. They're illegal here."

"It's not mine. It's yours." And he laughed and thanked me.

We were guarded by the US Marshals. I didn't mingle much because that made me think of bacteria.

"Sara, come down to the Marshals' office," said Mr. Edwards on the other end of my telephone. *Uh-oh. Do they know? Should I leave and go where I told Chaz to go, or should I just go downstairs and hold my breath?*

As I slowly made my way through the hallways of our courthouse, I wondered if my past was finally catching up with me. *But I can't think about that,* I said to myself. *Keep positive thoughts, but stay close to the exit doors.*

I hesitated.

The Marshals' door opened as someone was leaving.

"Sara." Mr. Edwards was waiting for me. "Come in and have a seat." He waved me over.

I thought for sure they were following a lead on the Senator, may he rest in pieces.

"Working with your judge," said Mr. Edwards, "you're going to have to get your security clearance."

"And what exactly does that mean?"

"Your judge has a high-profile courtroom, and you will be asked to work on terrorist cases and trials that are closed to the public that you won't be able to talk about. Do you think you can do that?"

He should know, I thought.

"Fill out this application, and we'll take it from here."

Oh, boy.

"We'll interview your family, friends, and neighbors, and then we'll be in touch."

Well, for sure, I won't list Uncle Tony and the unorganized crew for references. I thought I outsmarted them by listing my judge in Arizona and the kids…who knew nothing!

When I left Mr. Edwards's office, I was able to breathe again. "This is majestic," I said to another court reporter going up on the elevator.

After a while, I got my security clearance and started working on hearings involving terrorists. In fact, one terrorist was so bad that in conversation with the Marshal who was assigned to our courtroom, I said, "Marshal, let's be sensible. Can't you take him in the back and shoot him? Just say he tried to escape."

"Sara, you know I'd love to do that, but I can't."

"Well, how about if I bring him to his cell, and I'll do it?"

No dice.

The next day, my judge called me in. "Sara, we have a special hearing this afternoon on a sealed case." By this time, I was educated. I knew if it's a sealed case, I better keep my mouth shut.

"Will it be interesting?"

"Yes, it will be interesting. And the courtroom will be closed and locked."

This was starting to sound like I may be able to learn something for, you know, my other job. "Can you tell me anything about it?" I asked.

"It's a group of young men who worked for a firm called Black Hawk. They were government contractors working in Baghdad, Republic of Iraq, and they shot some people in Nisur Square."

Oh, well, I thought. *I'm not going to learn anything from this. Maybe I should get them on the side and teach them a few tricks.*

Falls Church, Virginia

I still had my home in Sarasota, Florida, that I wanted to keep, but I also bought a three-story townhouse in Falls Church, Virginia. I made enough money at "my other job" in order to afford it. I figured the townhouse was close to DC. The TV show *JAG* was also filmed there. It's a nice little community. You drive off the main road, turn left, go down the hill, and there we were. One block of townhouses on each side of the street and the back door opened out into the woods with a little stream back there. What a nice place. I was awake very early one morning, looked outside, and saw a red fox.

Our block was interesting. The man across the street worked at the Office of Personnel Management, or OPM; the lady living next to him worked at the CIA; one worked for Homeland Security; one lady was recently retired from one of the oil companies in Saudi Arabia; and the lady next door to me was one of the original Vietnamese boat people.

"Joey." I still called him Joey. "Let's buy a hot tub for the back."

"I'm in."

The nicest part of that was sitting in the hot tub when it was snowing, and I'd close my eyes and think of the nights I slept in my husband's arms, and wish I could tell him all is forgiven.

Uh-Oh, FBI Calling

"I'm coming. I'm coming. Who is it?"

"FBI. We're looking for Sara Bocelli."

The first thought that came to mind was run downstairs, out the back door, and into the woods. But then what? I wonder what they want, and I thought of the time that I answered my door and the gentleman said, "IRS." And I said, "No, thank you," and shut the door. But this was the FBI.

"Can I help you?"

"Yes. May we come in?" they said as they held up their badges.

As they came in and sat down, the lady said, "We're investigating the murder of your ex-husband, Steven, and we'd like to ask you some questions."

"I'd be happy to answer your questions, but there's nothing much I know about it, other than somebody shot him at his house," I replied.

"Do you know of anyone he had a problem with, anyone you can think of that might go after him?" the male counterpart asked me.

"Yes," I said. "I know of many people that didn't like him. He worked up on the Indian Reservation in

Arizona a lot because he had a photography business. I don't think he had a very good reputation up there because he would come home on weekends and tell me about all the fights he would have with the men."

"Is there anyone in particular? Can you give us some names?"

"Oh no," I said. "I can't even pronounce most of the names. But if you go up to the reservation and show his photo, I'm sure they'll remember him. I don't know much about the incident because I left Arizona shortly after that and came back East. I'm working in Federal Court in DC." I figured maybe that would help me.

"Yes, we saw that in the file. And I understand you have your Top Secret SCI clearance?"

"I sure do."

"Did you have any reason to go back to the house, maybe to get your clothes, anything like that?"

"No, when I left the house, I took all my belongings and never went back."

"The neighbors described a shadow of someone around the house that night, and we're wondering if you were there, or if you know anything about that?"

"No, I didn't keep in touch with any of the neighbors or anyone else in Scottsdale. My kids came out to pick me up, and I never looked back, never spoke to anyone out there, and to tell you the truth, I was happy to get away from there. I'm sure you know the circumstances of our breakup. It was not an easy thing after my feet were broken, but I never saw him again after that except for the court hearing." *Insult intelligently*, I said to myself.

"Well, thank you for your cooperation. If you think of anything that might be worthwhile in our investigation, here's my card, please call and let me know."

"Sure," I said. "Good luck in your investigation."

They should know.

As soon as they left, the phone rang. *What the hell is going on here today?*

"Hello?"

"We have a problem. Can't talk about it now, but Billy and Max will be there tomorrow night after work."

"Okay, Unk."

I couldn't imagine what our "problem" was. *I swear, if I'm going to keep this up, I need a smaller gun.* This was like that movie I watched, *Married to a Wise Guy*. And then I thought, *Well, maybe they found the remains of our body dump in the swamps, but if they did, it had to be severely degraded and not recognizable. Now I better get my* culo (we pronounce it "koo-li") *into work so I'm not late.* That's the Italian word for "butt."

As I covered our sentencing that day in court with Mr. Knight (the defendant who had an insurance agency but was keeping all the money he took in from his clients, and as a result, they were not insured), I thought about what our "problem" might be.

"Good morning, Sara. How are you today?" Mr. Knight said to me as he entered the courtroom handcuffed and escorted by a US Marshal.

He was a nice man if it wasn't for that, always smiling, even as he was sentenced to prison for five years. But the judge said that because of his multiple mini strokes and brain damage, Mr. Knight could wait at home, confined to his house, until he was notified to report to prison. With all the money he was stealing from the insured, he bought a penthouse condo in DC that had an indoor pool. What a guy!

But two months later, I ran into Mr. Knight walking down the street in DC, and he came up to me and gave me a big hug. "Mr. Knight, what are you doing out of prison?" I said.

"They never notified me to report. I guess they forgot."

Well, you know what I did. I ran right back to the courthouse, through security, up the elevator into my judge's office, out of breath, and told him that Mr. Knight was still out on the street.

"What?" he said. "He was supposed to report months ago!"

He fixed that blunder right away.

The Grumps

The next night, the grumps, Billy and Max, who I was getting attached to, magically appeared at my house, and Billy tried to explain what happened, but he was not successful.

"Billy, I need more information. I shouldn't have to guess what you're saying when you're talking."

And Max, my little doll, was out of breath because he was so excited. "Sara," Max said, "do you have any...what do you call it? It's alcohol, and the word starts with a *D*."

"Max, do you mean moonshine?" Because I usually had moonshine in the house.

"That's it," he said.

I proceeded to pour them each a glass of moonshine, with peaches, as Max showed me an article from the local Jersey newspaper that read, "A somber crowd is ushered through the metal detectors and into the elevators that would take them up to Courtroom 600 of the US District Courthouse in Newark, New Jersey, where they await the appearance of three members of a New Jersey organized crime family charged with distributing drugs and running a high-end prostitution business."

"Billy, who was it?" was all I managed to communicate. I couldn't read any further. I was extremely happy this was not about our body dump of the Senator, Bobby Genovese, or the prince, or even my jackass ex-husband in Arizona, but it was in reference to some of the guys from our neighborhood.

"Word is one of the guys was sitting in a bar, got drunk, and started talking to undercovers. The more he drank, the more the idiot talked. He told them about a high-end whorehouse they were opening up, and then he sold them drugs. The idiot exchanged phone numbers with the undercovers, and they tapped his phone and had him followed."

"Who was it?"

"Some new guy Butch, and he involved Angelo and Mike."

"Oh, no," I said.

"Yeah, and talk is if they give up your uncle, they can make a deal."

"But they don't know anything. How can they deal?" I said, hoping the word wasn't out about my kills, or for that matter, Billy, Max, and my killing of the Senator.

"I don't know," said Billy. "Maybe Friday after work you can meet us down the Shore, and we'll see what we can find out."

"Okay. We have to investigate, maybe find Angelo and Mike and talk to them."

"I'm in," said Max. "Angelo and Mike have always been good to me, so let's do it. But what are we going to do? Is there an app for that?"

"The first thing we're going to do is find out who the undercovers are. We'll call Uncle Tony to send Injun and Mutsi to meet us in the area, and we'll go to the bar and see what we can find out. Billy, call some of the guys to start casing it out for us until we can get there."

"You got it."

"And find out more about this Butch character. I'm going to look into getting an electronic skeleton key in case we need something like that. I just did a trial where they used one to get into somebody's car. It unlocks the door and disables the alarm system. We'll stake out the bar, get a description of the undercovers and the car that they're using, and use the skeleton key to get in the car and see what we can find out."

"Yeah, then we'll hide in the car and choke them when they get in," Max said.

Billy asked, "But how will that help Angelo and Mike?"

"I don't know. Let me figure this one out," I told him.

Max said, "What's the definition of a will? It's a dead giveaway."

"Max, shut up," Billy said.

"A chicken crossing the road is poultry in motion."

"I have to drive home with him." Billy sighed.

9

Khobar Towers

The next day, I went to work, and we were having a court hearing on a bombing of the Khobar Towers, a terrorist attack on part of the US Air Force housing complex in Khobar, Saudi Arabia.

At one point in the hearing, they called a witness who was the brother of one of our men killed in the attack, and he was questioned by the attorney.

"Family loyalty was fundamental in our household. We were all to protect each other. My mom did her best in raising eight of us, and we, through Chris and Mary, were taught that we have to take care of each other and be loyal to family and always be there for one another."

I thought to myself, *This sounds like us.*

He continued testifying about how the family found out about their brother being killed in the attack.

Q: Okay. Now when did you first find out, sir, that there was a bombing at Khobar Towers?

A: At that time, I was working out of the house. It was late, I was working late and took a break from my office in the house just to catch up on the eleven o'clock news, and I had noticed there was a bombing. And Mike was also in the living room and went into the bedroom. I yelled to him, I said, "Mike, there's been a bombing over in Saudi." And I said, "I don't have a good feeling. Come and check it out." I didn't mention anything to Bill, at least, I didn't think I did."

Q: And when did you get the word that he had been killed?

A: It would have been earlier the next morning. I could have sworn it was five, four or five, six something."

Q: On June twenty-sixth?

A: Yes.

Q: Do you remember who called?

A: There was so much going on, I couldn't recall if it was Patrick or it was Mary. I tend to believe it was Patrick, but I'm not really sure.

Q: What was your first reaction?

A: I said, "Are you sure? Are you sure? Are you sure?"

Q: What was Billy's reaction?

A: Once I found out, I went in and woke up Michael and Billy, and they came out to the living room and said, "Are you sure it's Christopher?" I said, "That's what they say. Michael and I were talking, and Billy turned around and said, I got to be alone. I can't deal with this."

Q: He's a quiet individual, isn't he? Billy.

A: He's a big man with a really soft heart.

Q: So what did he do? He just went into his room and closed the door?

A: It was his way of dealing with it, yeah.

Q: What did all of you do the next day?

A: We were making arrangements to go to New York.

Q: And you all went up to New York. When you first saw your mother when you got up to New York, what was she like?

A: Crying. Distraught.

Oh my goodness, I thought. *I can't imagine something like this happening to my son.* Tears came to my eyes during his testimony. The interrogation continued.

> Q: At the wake, do you remember whether there were a lot of veterans there?
>
> A: That's what amazed me, the overwhelming number of veterans that showed up.
>
> Q: And some of these veterans didn't know the family, did they?
>
> A: Chris was a military man. He respected military life, and he would have really been happy to have seen his brethren, not family but military family, support him.

At this point, I was having difficulty holding back my tears. The testimony continued.

> Q: I would ask you to turn to Exhibit 142. What is that exhibit?
>
> A: This is the poem my brother Billy wrote to my brother Chris.
>
> Q: Would you read that poem? It's a very short poem.
>
> A: It's titled "American Flyer."

He started reading.

American Flyer going higher than anyone can see. You're my brother, and there's no other that I would rather see here today. So I could say don't ever go away. But now you're gone, and the fight is on to make it through each day. Wherever you go, you should know you're always on my mind. There's eight in pain that feel the same, that you were one of a kind. So, American Flyer, aim a little higher, and one day you will see you're not forgot and that you meant a lot. A hero you'll always be.

Love,

Your brother Bill

My nose was running, and my eyes were tearing; I was sobbing. Then the judge looked at me and said, "Sara, do you need a break?"

The courtroom was cleared, but the Marshals stayed behind to keep the courtroom safe. They were so dedicated.

"Mom, you on a break? What's the matter? Why are you crying?" Joey peeked in the back door because he saw the courtroom emptying out.

It came to be that when I was doing daily copy—that is, where I was working in a trial or hearing—and the attorneys wanted the transcript for the next day, Joey would come in, pick up my notes that I copied out on a disk for him, go into my office, put them in my office computer, and scope for me or work on the transcript. At the end of the day, I would read in final what he completed. We would print it up, put it together, and the attorneys would have it waiting in the courtroom for them the next day.

Saturday at the Jersey Shore

The trip from DC to Toms River was quiet. As I thought of Joey's dad, I cried my silent tears.

When I met up with Billy and Max, Brian was with them. Brian was in training with Billy, and Billy said, "Sara, we got news on the bar in Toms River where the hookup was. The crew checked it out, and the bartender is a friend of a friend who's connected. Your uncle wants us to make contact with her and see if she can describe the undercovers or if she knows anything about them."

Max said, "Simple. I'll grab the bartender, and if she doesn't tell us who her friend is that knows the undercovers, I'll give her the Kiss of Death."

Finding the bar, The Dungeon, was simple enough because Toms River is not a big town. Injun and Mutsi were already there waiting for us outside to give us an update on what they found out, and I said, "Hey, guys, let's go in and sit at the bar and order something to eat. I haven't had anything, and I'm hungry."

Oh, no. It's one of the girls I followed Bobby Genovese with, I thought. *But she doesn't know me and didn't see me, so I'm okay*, I thought. "Max, be nice. For now anyway."

"Hi, sweetheart. We all want a beer," said Billy as we sat down at the bar. "And when you have some free time, come on over and talk to me." She gave him a look of curiosity, and then he winked at her.

Oh, boy.

"Johnny G says he knows you," said Billy. "He said the beautiful lady behind the bar with the red hair. What's your name, beautiful? Or should I just call you Beautiful?"

"I'm Amy," said the redhead. "I know Johnny G, he's a good customer. What's your name?"

"My name is Sammy," said Billy as Max crossed his eyes and Brian started to smile. "Johnny G says you may be able to help us out. It would be worth it to you if you could. I understand you have a girlfriend who got hooked up with these two bikers that come to the bar, and she might be able to help us find them."

Amy said, "I don't want to get her in trouble."

"I got this," Max said.

"Hold it, Max," Billy told him. Amy had a concerned look on her face when she saw Max stand up, and she said to Billy, "Sammy, I don't want any trouble."

With that, Billy took out two thousand dollars in cash. Good thing the bar was empty because it was still early. "This is yours if you give us her name and address. She'll never know it came from you."

Bingo. Two thousand dollars did wonders in her world. Maybe she'd like a better job with me, I wondered. She proceeded to spill the beans. "I have a friend named Louise, who works at another bar called Louie's on the Boardwalk in Seaside Heights, and I can take you there if you wait until I get off work." Well, we didn't want to wait until midnight, so off we went to walk the Boards at the Jersey Shore and looked for Louie's Bar in Seaside Heights. *Back to my old stomping grounds*, I thought.

Driving from Toms River into Seaside Heights didn't take us very long.

Billy said to Max, "Hey, Max, watch where you're going. Don't drive over that grass. That looks like it's hysterical property."

I said, "No, Billy. You mean *historical*."

Max joined in the conversation, "No problem. For the record, my eyesight is 120 over 80."

This is going to be some trip, I thought.

When we finally reached Seaside Heights and found Louie's Bar, finding Louise was not difficult because we had a pretty good description of her from her so-called girlfriend, but talking to her was a little more difficult, so it was Max's turn.

I proceeded to go into the ladies' room to give Max some time to get acquainted with Louise, and when I got back to the table, I heard Louise say to Max, "I can't go out with you tonight. I have a boyfriend, and he's picking me up at midnight. And he's a Toms River detective and wouldn't like it very much if he found out."

"I won't tell him," Max said. "Tell you what...what's his name and address? I'll go ask him if I can take you out to dinner tomorrow night." Max was trying hard to find this detective. I just love him.

Away she walked. "I guess she's not going for it, Max," I said.

"Maybe I should tell her one of my jokes."

I continued, "Let's do this slowly until we can work it out anyway. We'll get a room somewhere tonight and stay over."

That night, our plan was coming together. "Maybe we're going at this the wrong way. Let's think from the end and work forward. They're going to need these two biker detectives to testify at the trial in order to get a conviction. Without their testimony, there's nothing. Let's go back to both places tomorrow night just to stay in touch, maybe get a look at the guy if he shows up. We have a little time." *And*, I thought, *I have to get back to DC to go to work on Monday.* We picked the jury for a trial starting with a defendant from Colombia who was a leader in an organization called the DARC and whom they call El Trinidado. "Supposedly"—you know, like "allegedly" as I was starting to understand this court language—the DARC captured some Americans and held them hostage.

The rest of the weekend was spent spying. Yep. Spying. We spent time at the bar in Seaside and spied, waiting for the detectives to show up but to no avail.

Maybe when I get back to DC, I can talk to some of the US Marshals and get some insight into more ways I can trap the detectives, not saying they trap anybody, but I'm sure they can give me some stories without realizing what they're telling me. What a nice bunch of guys.

Back at the Ranch

"All rise," the clerk said as the judge entered the courtroom.

The clerk said, "This is the case of the United States versus Jesus el Trinidado, criminal record 2015-0336. All parties are present at this time, Your Honor."

The Judge (the Court) said, "Sir, you may proceed."

The trial proceeded, and after a while, the defendant took the stand for direct examination. That afternoon, the federal prosecutor started his cross-examination of El Trinidado. "Could you explain to the jury how many Blocks are in the DARC?"

The defendant's answers were through a Spanish interpreter. "Seven."

"And the Eastern Block, just to clarify, there is an Estado Mayor Central of the entire DARC, correct?"

Oh, boy, I thought, *now I have to learn Spanish also.*

"Yes."

"Which, in English, would mean a Central General Staff?"

"Yes."

"And then there's an executive committee that is a subset of the Central General Staff called the Secretariat, correct?"

I thought to myself, *But this is a jungle gang we're talking about. Why all these high-end names for themselves?*

"Yes," said the defendant. "The Central General Staff will delegate responsibilities to the Secretariat."

"When you traveled to Quito in December, how many police and military hostages was the DARC holding?"

"I don't really remember the exact number, but I believe it was more than thirty."

"And you know the DARC had dressed up in military uniforms and lured Assembly members out of their offices with the threat of...with some sort of bomb threat, security threat, loaded them on buses, and took them into the jungle?"

"I did know that."

El Trinidado is putting his foot in his mouth, I thought to myself.

"And you knew that another person was kidnapped while he was out jogging, and another was abducted while he was in a United Nations vehicle by the DARC?"

"Yes."

"And looking at government's Exhibit Number 110, which is in evidence, this is a photo of Anita Bettino who was also kidnapped by the DARC ten days after this photo was taken. It was very clear by this photo at this meeting that it takes away from your credibility when you come to peace dialogues with machine guns across your lap, correct?"

"I don't remember that."

Oh, the shithead is finally catching on to shut up.

"You concede that people do not like being kidnapped by the DARC?"

"Of course."

I need a glass of wine, I said to myself.

The DARC, as I learned throughout the trial, was a guerrilla group in South America. I wonder if I can hire a few of them to grab these two detectives and take them back to the jungle with them.

10

Seaside Heights

The trial continued every day while I stayed in touch with Billy getting updates from Injun and Mutsi and what they were able to find out. Then on Thursday night, I called him, "Billy, just meet me tomorrow night in Seaside Heights. Our trial will be continuing on Monday with closing arguments, so I have to come back to DC Sunday night. I can drive myself after work, and this way I can stop and see my friend Larry, the one who used to be a professional wrestler. Maybe he can teach me some 'death holds.' Maybe not."

"Your Uncle Tony wants to know what's going on. He doesn't want to talk on the phone, so I'm keeping him updated. He wants you to be careful."

Okay, here we go. In the meantime, Injun and Mutsi spent the week between The Dungeon and the Boardwalk in Seaside Heights. Monmouth County where they lived wasn't far, so it was easy for them to commute back and forth.

On Saturday, we found Louise in Seaside and followed her right to her boyfriend detective after work.

"Billy," I said, "I brought Flunitrazepam with me."

"Flu who? Are you sick?"

"No, I'm not sick. It's used as a hypnotic or psychoactive drug. We can have fun with this."

"I don't know what you're talking about. How can I have fun?"

Then Max chimed in, "Let me go in and drag him out."

Then Brian said, "I'm all for it. Let's go, Max."

"Are you crazy?" Billy said.

"That's not relevant," Max replied.

"You two, we'll just wait for him to come out and follow him."

As we sat and waited and waited, Max entertained us. "Those who get too big for their britches will be exposed in the end."

At last, the door opened. "Let's get this over with," said Billy.

Max said, "Hey, I know the guy. That's Tommy B. I went to school with him." As Max started walking toward him, Tommy spotted him, put a stupid smile on his face, and walked over to us.

"Max, what are you doing here?"

"We just came to kidnap and torture you for information."

"You were always a funny guy, Max. Glad you haven't lost your—" With that, Billy hit him over the head.

"Billy—what the…what are you doing?" As Billy was wrapping a rope around Tommy to tie him up, Max told him, "Let me talk to him."

"Let's take him to the car first," I said.

"Max, what's going on?" Tommy managed to say as he was shaking his head.

"Here's what we need to know, Tommy. Two of our friends were taken into custody, and you were the detective. Angelo and Mike. We want to know everything."

"Max, I'm talking to you like a brother now. This guy Butch talked and talked about Angelo and Mike, and then he mentioned the Russian mob. We got word through our captain that the Russian mob is in town and trying to take over. Take this stupid rope off me so I can talk to you."

"Billy, do it." *I never heard Max speak with so much authority. He's growing into a wonderful mobster,* I thought. *Demanding. Organized.*

"So now we're trying to stop the Russians from opening up prostitution rings and drug houses when all of a sudden we hear about a murder plot."

"Yeah?" said Billy. "But what about Angelo and Mike? They ain't killing nobody. This Butch kid, that's the one you want."

"But these guys know Butch, and Butch knows about the murder. At first, we thought it was the Wise Guys, but it's not. It's the Russians. We just took Angelo and Mike in to try to get some info from them, try to scare them a little."

"But who's this guy that's supposed to get hit?"

"The Vice President."

Max looked at him with questionable eyes. "The vice president of what?"

"The Vice President of the United States."

"Are you out of your mind? Angelo and Mike ain't part of nothing like that. What's the matter with you?"

As Billy started pacing outside the car, Max was thinking. And me? I was just sitting there like a lady!

Max came to life. "Okay, here's what we're doin'. You take us to Angelo and Mike, let us talk to them, and we'll find out everything they know about this hit, and you get them released."

"Hey, man, I'll try, but it's not up to me."

Billy jumped in, "Well, you're staying with us until we can see them to talk. We want a deal!"

"Yeah," said Brian all of a sudden. I looked at Brian, what got into him?

Boy, I thought, *Billy has his course of action straight, but the detective hasn't done anything.* I didn't think he wanted to spend the night with us, so he enticed us to drive to Newark jail right then and there—in the middle of the night. "I'll call the captain to meet us there."

"Okay." I finally added to the conversation so Tommy didn't think I was a dead person sitting there. "Let's go." And we, as crazy people, went to the Newark jail.

Four Crazy People and a Fifth

Tommy took us into his captain's office, where the captain was unhappily sitting there waiting for us.

"Captain, this is Max. Max and I went to school together. He's a good guy."

"Hello," said the captain. "Nice to meet you. And you are?"

"Here. In the middle of the night," was Billy's response.

I quickly responded, "I'm Sara," to get the captain's attention away from smart-ass Billy. "This is Brian. Nice to meet you."

As Tommy partly explained to his captain the reason we were there in the middle of the night, leaving out the hit over the head and the rope tied around his body, I stayed in the background while Max took over. "These guys wouldn't do something like putting out a hit on the Vice President," said Max. "They're good guys. They got families. We know them. They wouldn't do that."

"I can't get into detail with you, but we know the Russian mob is involved," responded the captain.

"Well, Captain," I said. "I have my top secret security clearance, SCI. And as you know, SCI is Sensitive Compartmented Information. Perhaps we can talk."

I followed him to another room, where he checked on my credentials. He checked with the FBI, and they even put a call in to my judge at that hour of the morning, who confirmed who I was. Face Time is amazing. I think the captain was amazed and shocked that I was telling the truth. I didn't tell him anything about my other job, though, you know, the killing one. We continued to talk about the planned hit on the Vice President, and hours turned into breakfast.

Thereupon (you like that word?), Butch, Angelo, and Mike were brought into different rooms for questioning. The captain wanted to take it one step at a time, come to find out Angelo and Mike only heard Butch mention it, but thought he was crazy.

Butch was the one. He had all the information. So now what to do? We needed to set up a trap to capture the bad guys—the Russians, the Russian mob who thought they were going to come into our country and take over. *We'll get rid of those bastards*, I thought, *and all with the help of the police captain. Funny how that works, isn't it?*

"But we'll need more help," I said. "I have a friend who may be willing to help save the Vice President." I was thinking of Chaz. "But you have to exonerate him from any crime or any investigation you have going on with him."

"Sara," the captain said. I guess now we were on first names. I mean, I just spent the night with him. "I have to check this guy out first."

"No, you don't. Let me call him. He'll come in and talk and see what we come up with first. If we can't think of a plan and you can't use him, well, that's all right too. If you think you can use him, of course, he'll give you his name. He doesn't have SCI clearance, but I'm sure he'll be helpful to you."

"*Princesa*," Chaz said when I called him early in the morning. "Nice to hear from you, but the sun's not even up yet."

"Chaz, can you come to Newark Detention Center? Right now? Somebody will meet you downstairs to bring you up."

"Are you in trouble? How much is the bail?"

"No, handsome. Just bring yourself, and you'll be okay up here. Don't worry about it."

Now I had to go out and tell Max and Billy what was going on. Brian was waiting outside in the car. We needed more coffee. This was a long night, and I thought it was going to continue longer than expected. Why didn't I mind my own business? But why in the world did the Russian mob want to kill our Vice President? Why not the President? I couldn't figure that one out. Butch didn't know why either, but maybe we could find out.

While we waited for Chaz, we ordered bagels with salmon and cream cheese and more coffee and actually enjoyed our wait at the detention center.

"*Princesa.*"

Oh, boy. This is going to be fun, I thought as I introduced him to the captain and explained to him that Butch, Angelo, and Mike were all in separate rooms. They were questioned and still being held. We went on to talk, and Chaz replied to the captain, "So what do you want from me? I don't know anything."

"Here's the thing, Chaz. If we can come up with a plan, you'll be exonerated, and they'll stop all investigations of you."

"Forever?"

"No, sweetheart, but up to now they will."

"First thing we gotta do," he said, "is talk to Butch. Find out where he got this info and who he got it from. Next thing we gotta do, *princesa*, is get more of the guys working on this. We need Frank, Angelo, and Mike working with us, not sitting in jail. I don't care what they do with Butch."

I looked at the captain. "No," he replied.

"Okay, bye-bye." As I looked into his beautiful cold blue eyes, I could tell he was full of baloney, but the captain couldn't tell because he didn't know him. I went along with it. "Okay, sorry it didn't work out, Chaz. See you."

And the captain jumped in, "Hold on, you two. Just calm down. Don't get excited. Maybe we can work something out. I'm going to go in and question Butch again, and you—whatever your real name is—stay here with Sara and listen. Tell me if you pick up something from the conversation."

The captain went in and questioned Butch some more; he talked a little bit more this time about the Russians than he did last time, where he was when he heard what was going to happen, who he was with. The captain told him that he was trying to work things out and asked if he would be willing to cooperate, blah, blah, blah. Then Big Blue Eyes Chaz smiled, and his eyes lit up. "Did he just mention meeting them at an Italian-American feast? The Feast of San Gennaro is starting up tomorrow, and I was reading in the newspaper that the Vice President will be there."

We quickly knocked on the door to get the captain out—some would call it banging on the door excitedly. Then Chaz explained to the captain his thoughts, and if he was right, it would be happening tomorrow evening in Little Italy during the feast.

"Okay, exonerate me," Chaz told the captain. "We have things to do. I need Sara, Billy, Max, Frank, Angelo, and Mike with me. I don't care what you do with Butch. Tommy B can come with us and a few more of your men that Tommy trusts. I have friends that live down there, and we'll spread the word about the hit."

"I can't be having mass confusion down there. That won't work," said the captain.

"It will work if you tell your men not to pull out their guns and shoot anybody. That will be the mass confusion. We'll circulate through the crowd, keep our eyes open, and take them down. You just tell your men not to shoot into the crowd. Don't even tell the Secret Service because then it will really be mass confusion."

We then brought in Tommy and got Angelo and Mike out of lockup. Tommy picked four of his most trustworthy guys, and when we were all together, the captain went over the plan. I had to get out of there to call Uncle Tony. He needed to know this wasn't an investigation against him, and I was sure it would make him feel better.

"Captain, I'll be right back. Have to use the restroom," I said as I started out the door looking for my phone.

"Hi, Unk, it's me. Just checking in." I started telling him briefly, very briefly, about what was happening. "Yes, Unk, we'll be working with the government to protect the Vice President of the United States!"

Oops! I better include myself in that exoneration deal.

"I'm proud of you," he said as we hung up the phone.

I made my way back to "the room" where everyone was and told the captain that Billy, Max, Brian, and I hadn't slept yet and needed a few hours of sleep before we get cranky, although I was sure Brian was out in the car snoozing. The captain informed me that he called my judge back and that I didn't have to go into work on Monday and that he would get another court reporter in to do the closing arguments. What a guy! We all confirmed we'd meet up at four o'clock that afternoon in the captain's office, while Billy, Max, Brian, and I left to grab a nap, and Chaz went downtown New York to "take care of business."

Taking Care of Business

By the time we got to the feast that night, Chaz had everything under control. He had a gang of giants together. They must have been ten foot tall and weighed five hundred pounds each, and they were ready! Now all the detectives got to meet them so they wouldn't be shot, and Chaz reminded them not to pull out their weapons. He also reminded the captain that he and I were both exonerated. No mistakes made. Organized crime was now working with the government to get the Russians under control. Got it?

"Spread out!" Chaz shouted. He was in control... I guess!

Chaz's monsters started walking around Little Italy, mingling. (There's that nasty word again.) They knew so many people down there—big ones, little ones, and those in-between. As they walked, they talked, making all their friends aware to look out for the Russians. As everyone was spreading the word, they were also downloading the Panic Button onto their cell phone so that when the bad guys are spotted, you just press the Panic Button and then they could text in their location for the rest of us to know where they were. After all, Little Italy is a quaint little place.

"Captain, your men better not shoot any of my men, or they won't get out of Little Italy alive." Chaz was threatening the captain out of love.

Sunset finally came. I thought of the beautiful sunsets on Siesta Beach and Engelbert's "Time Goes By So Slowly."

"Sara," I heard Chaz call me. "You better stay with me. Your mind is wandering." Boy, not only could we read each other's mind, but he was still taking care of me.

"Frank, where are you?" I yelled.

"I'm right behind you," I heard him respond. "And I see Billy the Kid and Max and Brian." We were all trying to stay close.

And then we heard the band playing, people singing "America the Beautiful." *Something's up*, I thought, *with Chaz on one side of me and Frank on the other*. We saw the truck-driven float coming by with balloons, playing loud music, and I thought this was it. If somebody would shoot at our Vice President, nobody would hear the shot until it was too late, and we'd never know where the shot came from. But that was no good. We had to stop the shooter or shooters before they would shoot.

The Vice President was up there smiling and waving at everybody. We were never able to find out on such short notice what he did to have the Russians go after him, but I didn't care. I figured we'd be exonerated. Mark this date on the calendar.

"Let's follow the float," said Frank. After all, there was nothing happening yet.

As the three of us walked together, not like the Three Stooges but more like The Avengers, we could see Angelo and Mike on the other side of the float. We could see the monsters all over—actually big monsters—and by this time, there were also little monsters. We could see the captain's men and, of course, the Secret Service swarming around the Vice President, who knew nothing about what was going on. Never had I witnessed an attempted murder as enormous as this. The Vice President and the Secret Service were unsuspecting souls of a possible catastrophic event.

But wait, nothing was happening!

We were approaching the end of the parade boundaries, and still nothing was happening. Something was wrong. The Vice President was still waving and smiling. Something was definitely out of play here.

So The Avengers moved quietly into place and close to the Vice President, keeping in mind our exoneration. All of a sudden, Chaz pressed the Panic Button; he didn't have to text where we were because everybody else was in reach of the Vice President.

Our gang stayed together and quickly followed Chaz toward the alleyway because the Vice President was heading toward that direction. Everybody else was concentrating on the Vice President, but now our gang was concentrating up ahead.

A monster, a big monster, one of Chaz's monsters, spotted three Russians and made his way quickly toward them. *What a big guy*, I thought, *except he's not green. Don't big guys like this have green skin and red eyes?* Well, Chaz's monster grabbed one Russian in each hand, and it looked like he was dangling them up in the air. *Holy smoke,* I thought. There were three Russians, but what happened to the third? He disappeared.

"Okay, put the bad guys down," said Chaz.

Billy said, "Give me them. Let me shoot them."

"No. We need exoneration. Or maybe I should shoot them because my exoneration includes today. I don't care why they wanted to kill the Vice President," who was actually still standing there smiling and waving. He had no idea what was going on, and still neither did his Secret Service agents who were guarding him so closely. All of a sudden, the captain was in the midst of our gang, so all thoughts of corruption, torture, and murder were immediately ceased. *But where did the third Russian go?* I thought.

As the captain stepped in, he and his men took a hold of the two Russians, quietly handcuffed them so nobody knew a massacre had almost taken place of our Vice President, and took them into the alleyway to be searched.

"You can't search me," said one Russian to the captain.

"I'm not going to search you," said Max. "What started out as a search will now progress one step further to a murder. I'm going to choke you."

Oh my. Thankfully Tommy B stepped in.

"Tommy," I said. "There were three Russians. We only have two."

"I'll have our guys search the alleyway and keep their eyes open."

We all watched as the two Russians were searched, and hidden away under their jackets were a Russian AK-47 with a pistol grip and a short-barreled shotgun. In their pockets were also switchblades, and they both had a Kubotan attached to their key ring. Well, could you guess what they were up to? I hoped they would never be seen or heard of again.

The search for the missing third Russian continued while the Vice President was waving and smiling. Tommy's men were in the alleyways searching in the garbage bins in case the Russian was trying to hide in one, and two of the detectives lowered a fire escape ladder to go up and search the roof of the building. But the third Russian just mysteriously vanished.

The captain was thankful that we were able to catch the two Russians before the Secret Service got to them and all hell broke loose. He and his men quietly dragged them out of there as the Vice President continued waving and smiling and the Secret Service watched for danger as the parade ended.

As long as I didn't have to go to work in the morning, I told the captain we'd all be in his office tomorrow for our amnesty papers.

"What? It was only you and Chaz," said the captain.

"How about Billy and Max?" I asked him, knowing Brian didn't commit any murders yet. "We couldn't have done it without them." I figured if the Senator was ever found and identified, Billy and Max would also be free and clear. "They really have nothing to exonerate, but just in case."

"I'll see you all tomorrow morning in my office."

As we were preparing to leave, Max said to the captain, "Did you hear about the man who fell into an upholstery machine?"

And the captain replied, "Yeah. He was fully recovered."

Before Chaz's monsters left, I was going to ask the biggest one. "Did your mother give you Grow-Pup? How in the world did you get this big?" But then I thought never mind. It may be something I'd be unable to forget.

We checked into a hotel for the night close by the detention center in Newark. What a bad neighborhood this was. *Well, no thugs better try to mug us, or they'd be sorry*, I thought. On the other hand, maybe it would be fun. But our gang checked in, and we all stayed together as usual. There's strength in numbers.

The next day, on our way to the captain's office to get our amnesty papers, Max started to say, "Two peanuts were walking down the street. One was as-salted."

"Are we there yet?" asked Billy. "Stop for the red light when you stop."

The captain was very happy to see us. He welcomed us all, looked at Max, and said, "Hey, Max, did you see the sign in the cafe down the street that said, 'Buy one dog, get one flea?'"

"Oh, that's a good one," said Max. "I'll have to remember that."

The captain then brought us into an adjoining room where the rest of his team was waiting. "Let me have your attention, everybody. Don, quiet down...As you all know, we had a pretty demanding and nerve-racking day yesterday. Our Vice President was in danger of being either killed or kidnapped by three Russians, and with the help of our civilian team over here, we managed to save the day and save our country from a disaster with Russia.

"We captured and brought in two men who belonged to the Russian mob. There were three altogether, but unfortunately, the third one escaped, but we will continue looking for him. We have some witnesses who can identify him, and they're with the artist now who's making up a profile of him so we can put him on the Most

Wanted list. I'd like to present my friends here with the Public Safety Officer Medal of Valor for saving the life of the Vice President of the United States."

"Oh my goodness!" Then I said to Tommy, "Wait until Joey hears about this!"

We all stood up to receive our awards, and I said, "There's one more man out there, and we won't stop looking for him until he's found."

And Max joined in with, "Is there an app for that?" which, of course, started the place in laughter.

Afterward, I went home to my townhouse in Falls Church, Virginia, and drove defensively as Victor used to tell me.

Maybe it's time to take a vacation and go back down to Sarasota and spend some time on Siesta Beach.

"Hello." my cell phone rang.

"Hi, babe. Got a job for you."

"Okay. See you tomorrow, Unk."

"I'm very proud of you."

That night when I went to bed, I put my head on the pillow, and as I closed my eyes, I thought of my husband, my love.

"I sleep in your arms, and All Is Forgiven."